Marissa Moss

Mira's Diary

LOST IN PARIS

MARISSA MOSS

sourcebooks
jabberwocky

Text and illustrations copyright © 2012 by Marissa Moss
Cover and internal design © 2012 by Sourcebooks, Inc.
Original series design by Liz Demeter/Demeter Design

Sourcebooks and the colophon are registered trademarks of Sourcebooks, Inc.

Published by Sourcebooks Jabberwocky, an imprint of Sourcebooks, Inc.
P.O. Box 4410, Naperville, Illinois 60567-4410
(630) 961-3900
Fax: (630) 961-2168
www.jabberwockykids.com

Library of Congress Cataloging-in-Publication data is on file with the publisher.

Source of Production: Bang Printing, Brainerd, Minnesota, USA
Date of Production: July 2012
Run Number: 18265

Printed and bound in the United States of America.
BG 10 9 8 7 6 5 4 3 2 1

To all who dare to speak out against injustice

"Injustice anywhere is a threat to justice everywhere."
—*Martin Luther King Jr.*

JuNe 11

Who sends postcards anymore? I wondered when I saw it in the mailbox. How quaint, how old-fashioned. The picture was an old black-and-white photo of a gargoyle on Notre Dame Cathedral in Paris, the kind you might find in a musty antique shop. Even the faded French stamp looked like it was from a previous century. Then I recognized the loopy handwriting and

my stomach lurched, first in relief, then in boiling hot rage. So Mom wasn't dead, kidnapped, or suffering from amnesia. She was gone, plain and simple.

Dear David, Malcolm, and Mira,

I know this has been a shock to you all, but don't worry about me. I'm doing what I should have done years ago. There is so much I need to learn, but believe me I'll be home as soon as I've figured things out.

Gargoyles have always fascinated me. Just think what stories they could tell if we only spoke their language!

Take care of yourselves, and remember that I love you.

Serena (Mom)

I examined the card—front, back, and sideways—but that was it. She'd left us, and all she said was "don't worry about *me*"? I was furious! Such a tra-la-la, have-a-nice-day kind of message when she'd thrown a bomb into our lives, blowing our family apart.

When we first realized Mom was really gone, I was terrified. We called the cops, filed a missing person report, waited with our breath held, and…nothing. A big fat nothing. Funny how quickly I went from being scared that she'd been hurt to wanting to kill her myself.

Dad was a wreck. He expected to get ransom demands from

some mythical kidnappers for weeks. Every time the phone rang, he'd practically jump out of his socks. As the weeks rolled by and he corralled us into therapy, he talked about Mom as if she was on one of her work trips that she'd somehow forgotten to tell us about. She didn't answer her cell phone? The battery must have died. No email? She must be super busy. But after months went by, even Dad couldn't believe his own lie.

Still he swore he didn't have a clue that Mom was unhappy or that she wanted out of our family. He insisted something else had to be going on. Like what, my brother, Malcolm, and I wanted to know. Like Mom's really a secret agent and she's on some hush-hush mission?

Malcolm is sixteen, a couple of years older than me, and his humor kept me from crying my eyes out those first days. Some people think he's too sharp, but to me his sharpness has a reason. Plus, he isn't mean, just scathingly right. He's awkwardly tall and skinny, too smart to be cool, with unruly hair he proudly calls a Jewfro. Looking like that, you need a sense of humor.

Mom says he's just like her dad, with that same drive to succeed, that same need to prove himself, but minus the skill as a sculptor since that's what Grandpa did. I always thought Malcolm was her favorite. He gets better grades, takes harder classes, and actually thinks math is fun. So I knew Mom didn't want to abandon Malcolm. Me, I wasn't so sure about.

Secretly I always wondered if Mom was disappointed in me.

I'm not beautiful like her, though Dad says I'm cute (but then, what father doesn't say that about his daughter?). Mom's face is a smooth oval, her hair wavy, her eyes big and golden. I have her eyes, but that's about it. I'm short, with wild kinky hair and a nose a little too big for my face. Kind of like Dad, I guess, but minus the John Lennon glasses.

What I really wanted to inherit was artistic ability. Not Mom's, but her father's, the one Malcolm is like. Grandpa was such a successful sculptor that he even had pieces in big museums. And Dad is an artist too with his photography. I try, but I can never get on paper what I see in my head. So instead of talent, all I've gotten from Mom is a tendency for dark circles under my eyes. And now this postcard.

Dad didn't have any answers, but he said Mom loved us, would always love us, and someday we'd learn the truth about why she left. Someday, as soon as she could, she'd come back to us. I wanted to believe him, but it sounded so lame. Malcolm was probably right—Mom had a boyfriend we didn't know about and she'd decided to leave with him and not even say good-bye. No note, no phone call, no email even. Until six months after her disappearing act, this postcard came in the mail.

When I showed it to Malcolm, he was just as steamed.

"She's having café au lait in Paris so she can study gargoyles? What kind of excuse is that? What isn't she saying—that she has a French boyfriend? Ooh-la-la!"

"I know," I said. "She acts like this is an itty-bitty bump in the road, not a slap in the face." I slumped into the big overstuffed chair that Mom used to cuddle with us in, used to read books to us in. I thought I knew her. She was my mother, after all. Now she sounded like a chirping stranger. I left the postcard on the kitchen counter with the rest of the mail for Dad to find. And I tried to forget about it, to forget about her.

But that postcard really got Dad going. He was sure it was a message. Slamming cupboards, chopping onions, he started making dinner in the noisiest way possible. That meant he was super excited. Whenever he won an award for one of his photographs, the kitchen looked like an explosion had happened, but it was just Dad making meat loaf to celebrate. That says something about Dad—that he thinks meat loaf is festive. Why was he celebrating now?

"This isn't an explanation at all. And it doesn't sound like your mother. Something weird is going on here. I know it!" Dad stirred the spaghetti sauce as if he could read the answer in its thick bubbles. "She doesn't sound safe. She's in trouble, or she wouldn't *not* ask about you guys."

Okay, maybe it wasn't a celebration, but Dad didn't sound mad either. He was worried, but more than that, he actually sounded happy. Could you be happy and worried at the same time?

Malcolm set the table while I tossed the salad. If I let Dad near the tongs, there'd be lettuce all over the place.

"C'mon, you two!" Dad said. "You can't believe your mother would leave you for such a frivolous reason!"

"Define 'frivolous,'" Malcolm said. "If you mean flighty, flimsy, flitty, I'd agree. I can't see Mom dumping us for a stone monster. Even one in Paris. But if you mean Mom's covering up her real reason, which could possibly be just as stupid, I'd buy that."

Dad set the bowl of spaghetti on the table and poured himself a glass of wine. We sat down like it was a normal family dinner. Like it was every day that we got a message from our missing mother.

"Let's be logical about this, think about what we do know instead of guessing about things we don't. Do we want Mom back with us?" Dad looked at me, but I couldn't meet his eyes. To tell the truth, I wasn't sure. Of course, I loved her and I missed her, but my anger was bigger than both those things. How could I ever trust her again?

"Do we?" Dad pressed.

Malcolm shrugged. "I guess. But she has a *lot* of explaining to do. And this postcard doesn't cut it."

"Okay, but we want to give her a chance. We want to be able to forgive her, right?"

I nodded. I could admit that much.

"Good!" Dad forked up a glob of spaghetti like he'd suddenly realized he was starving. His eyes lit up like he'd hit pay dirt, not pasta. "That means we're going to Paris!"

"Paris!" I squawked.

"Paris?" Malcolm echoed. "When? What about school? Work?"

"That's my news," Dad said. "I was going to tell you right away, but then there was the postcard. I got that fellowship I applied for, the one to photograph the Wonders of the World."

I guess I should explain here that Dad's a professional photographer. He's known for his aerial views, but this past year he's been working on a new project. He wants to select and explore a whole new series of architectural wonders. In ancient times, there were seven wonders. He thinks now there are probably twenty or so, including things like the Golden Gate Bridge, the Great Wall of China, Machu Picchu, places the Greeks couldn't know about because they didn't exist yet.

He wants to come up with a new list and then photograph them all so we'll appreciate and understand the wonders around us. Plus it's a great excuse to travel to cool places and see amazing things. That's what he told us when he was working on the grant application, but I have to admit, I never thought he'd get it.

"That's great news!" I said, though I wasn't sure it was. I wanted to be happy for Dad, but this was all really weird.

"And since Mom's in Paris, that's the first place we'll go. I'll have to decide which wonder to focus on, Notre Dame or the Eiffel Tower. What do you guys think?"

"We're going with you?" Malcolm asked.

"Well, I can't leave you here by yourselves. I'll homeschool you for the year. Besides, you'll learn a lot just going to the places I'm photographing."

"A whole year?" I didn't mind the idea of no school for a year, plus we would travel all over the world. But I wasn't crazy about leaving my friends behind. And I didn't believe the part about finding Mom or learning the truth about why she left. Right now I just wanted to forget her. The same way she'd obviously forgotten about us.

Malcolm raised his glass of milk. "A toast to Dad, his fellowship, and a year of travel! When do we leave? I can be packed in five minutes." He clearly didn't care about missing his friends, even though he spent every free minute with them. Maybe boys are fickle like that.

"Is this definitely decided?" I asked. "It's so sudden."

"You know I've been working on this idea for a while," Dad said. "I guess you didn't have faith I'd actually get the grant."

"That's not it," I muttered. Though it sort of was.

"She's afraid she'll miss the glories of junior high," Malcolm teased. "Don't worry. I'll tell you all about it and you'll feel like you're there."

"I don't want your school experience. I want mine."

"Mira, is this really a problem?" Dad put on his concerned *how are you* face, one of my least favorite expressions, right after *because I say so*.

"No, Dad, of course not." How could I add to his disappointment? I didn't want to be like Mom, letting my family down. "It's great. I'm sure my friends will keep me posted on what's going on. There's email in France, isn't there?"

Dad grinned. "Despite the old-fashioned postcard, there is."

And that's how we ended up going to Paris.

July 1

It felt strange to be traveling without Mom, being on a huge plane, landing in a foreign country, having my new passport stamped for the very first time. I was so excited to see the billboards in French as we drove from the airport into the city, and then we were there, breezing alongside the Seine in the morning sunshine, turning down small winding streets until the cab pulled up outside our hotel. We were in Paris, which was already extraordinary, so I guess it was normal that nothing was normal. This was our family checking into our hotel—just me, Malcolm, and Dad.

I tried not to think about Mom, to think about Paris instead, noticing the art deco metro entrances, the woman walking down the street with a baguette under her arm, just like you would see in the movies, the total Frenchness of our hotel. Dad had chosen a charming, tiny hotel, in the Place Sainte-Catherine in the heart of the Marais. The beds took up most of the room, so we just dumped our suitcases, eager to be out in the streets, to soak up Paris. Dad slung his camera over his shoulder, Malcolm carried the city map, and I took my sketchbook, the small one I could tuck into my pocket.

Marais means "swamp" and during the Middle Ages, this whole area on the right bank of the Seine was a giant marsh. Since it was clearly the worst place to live in the city, it was also the Jewish ghetto. There were still little hole-in-the wall synagogues, bakeries that sold challah and skinny French-Jewish bagels, and plaques all over the place marking the spots where Jewish families were rounded up and shipped off to concentration camps during World War II.

I could see the plaques and bagels myself. The other stuff I learned from Malcolm. He reads constantly and his favorite subject is history. If history was the only topic on *Jeopardy*, Malcolm could go on the show and win a fortune. That's how much he knows.

Dad, on the other hand, is a read-the-guidebook-right-before-you-see-anything kind of guy. "This may have been a mosquito-ridden marsh centuries ago, but now it's a trendy neighborhood. Look at all these pricey boutiques!" He pointed out a chi-chi clothing store (which of course we did *not* go into) right next to a dingy orthodox synagogue that was smaller than Arinell's, the tiny joint that makes our favorite pizza back home in Berkeley. You could just squeeze a minyan inside, the ten men necessary for Jews to pray together. I couldn't imagine the bent-over men with wispy gray beards, dressed in their long black coats, walking into the brightly lit shop next door with blaring French rap music and neon mannequins strutting in the windows. Talk about a culture clash.

"It's a different kind of ghetto now is all, an upscale one," Malcolm said. Totally wasted on him, I thought. Some guys actually cared about making a fashion statement, but not him.

And to be honest, I wasn't much good at it either. I wear jeans and T-shirts as much as he does.

We were meandering around on our first day in Paris, just getting a feel for the city, but really I think we were all looking for Mom, expecting to see her every time we turned a corner.

Dad led the way across the Seine to an island in the middle of the broad river. French schoolchildren on a field trip, their voices high and piping, crowded the narrow street. I wondered where they were going but as the street opened onto a square, I could see what drew them, what had attracted tourists from around the world and throughout the centuries. Notre Dame Cathedral. The home of the gargoyle on Mom's postcard.

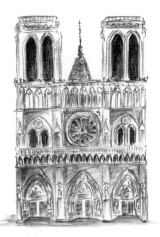

We live in California, a young state in a young country, so about the oldest thing you can see there, besides the ancient redwood groves, is Sutter's Fort near Sacramento, where gold was discovered in 1848. Notre Dame was built seven centuries before that! It's an enormous, broad-shouldered building with elegant arches and flying buttresses pulling it up to the sky. Dad was right—it's truly a wonder of the world.

Beautiful sculptures of prophets and apostles line deep portals on either side of the three massive front doors. Arches over the doors are also filled with sculptures, stories from the Bible carved in stone. I stood gaping, trying to figure out what the stories were. For a second, I imagined Mom standing in this exact same spot, head

tipped back, reading the stones, and I felt a pang. She might have been here. Maybe she still was.

Usually when you go into a building, it's lighter or darker, cooler or warmer than outdoors, but it's still part of the same world. Stepping into Notre Dame was like changing time zones or countries, crossing some magical border. A hush filled the cavernous, echoey space of the cathedral, despite all the voices of tourists murmuring and people praying, as if the sound was absorbed into the bones of the building itself.

Light streamed in from the windows like a physical presence, the kind of light you think you can reach out and touch. I couldn't resist running my fingers over the brilliant colors cast onto the floor by the stained glass. I felt like  I could pick them up, collect them in my hands. The air itself felt still and chilled by the stone all around. The walls were stretched thin between the pillars that soared into a vault overhead, like the skin of a massive beast taut between its ribs.

"Come on," Malcolm whispered. "Let's light a candle for Mom."

"Why?" I asked, annoyed that he'd jarred me out of the peaceful rhythm of the cathedral. "She isn't dead, just gone."

But the flickering flames of the long white candles

mesmerized me. I wanted to light one for myself. I didn't have any euros yet, but I slipped some quarters into the slotted metal box, lit a candle from the flame of its brother, and impaled it on one of the metal spikes branching out in front of a side altar. I wondered how many people had done this same simple thing and what they'd prayed for. A good harvest, a healthy baby, a new cow? I knew Malcolm was praying for Mom to come back, but I wasn't sure I wanted that. Would I forgive her if she called us tomorrow, said she was sorry for leaving?

I stared into the flames, searching for what I really wanted. An answer. I prayed to know the truth—good, bad, or ugly. I wanted to know why.

Dad found us standing there, his guidebook open in his hands.

"Lose the book," I begged. "You're making us look like dumb tourists."

"We are dumb tourists, and this book is useful. It says here that you can climb a tower to go out to a walkway above the roof where the gargoyles are lined up. Let's find the one from Mom's postcard."

"You think Mom's waiting for us there?" Malcolm rolled his eyes. He's an expert eye-roller, believe me.

"Of course not! I like gargoyles, that's all." Dad tucked the guidebook into the messenger bag slung over his shoulder. "And I'll speak to you in French so we won't seem like tourists."

"You don't have to go that far," I said. My French is pretty basic. *Bonjour, merci,* and *je m'appelle Mira.* Dad's wasn't much better. Mom was fluent. But she wasn't here.

We went outside to join the line that snaked alongside the flank of the cathedral. The last time I'd been in a line like this was at Great America, waiting to get on the Ultimate Drop ride. Now I was climbing a narrow, twisting stairway in a Gothic tower but I was just as nervous, scared almost. It was stupid to think we'd find Mom next to some gargoyle. Or a hidden message. But I couldn't get rid of the feeling that we were closer to her, that something was about to happen that would change everything.

After the cramped darkness of the tower, it was a relief to be out on the walkway. The view was amazing. All Paris lay spread out before us, the Seine river, bridges crisscrossing it, the towers of the fortress-like Conciergerie where nobles were imprisoned during the French Revolution, the Eiffel Tower, Gothic spires and slate roofs. It looked like something from a Madeline

book. I almost expected to see nuns leading two straight lines of little girls dressed in blue and white with black hats perched on their heads.

All along the walkway,

stone monsters crouched. In most churches gargoyles were fancy gutters, covering the spouts that channeled rainwater away from the walls. In Notre Dame, the gargoyles were simply decoration. Dad suggested they might be there to protect the cathedral from evil spirits. To me, they looked like evil spirits themselves. Still, I couldn't resist drawing them.

"Why have creepy creatures on a church? It's like inviting demons rather than repelling them," I said. "Why did Mom pick a gargoyle postcard?"

"She's protecting us from evil, obviously," Malcolm drawled.

"Don't make fun that way," Dad said. "Maybe she really is. You don't know."

"You don't either," Malcolm snapped. "You just want to forgive and forget."

I didn't want a fight. Malcolm thought Dad was a doormat, letting Mom step all over him. Dad thought Malcolm was rushing to judge what he didn't understand. I thought they should both shut up. After all, we were in Paris, Mom or no Mom.

It seemed safer to walk away than try to stop them, so I squeezed past and studied the weird creatures perched on the edge of the walkway. Some gargoyles looked like bird-beasts, others like lion or wolf creatures. And there, right in front of me, was the one from

Mom's postcard, a really creepy humanoid, reptilian thing with a stubby unicorn horn.

I knew you weren't supposed to touch the art, but I couldn't help myself. I felt drawn to the jutting brow, the goatish beard. The thing seemed so real, as if the demonic eyes would blink any minute. I reached out a finger and touched its shoulder, expecting the warmth of something alive. But the stone was cold, searingly cold, like ice. A shock ran through me as if I'd touched an electrical socket.

Now this is the freaky part, and I'm not sure how to explain it. When I touched that gargoyle, I saw flashes of it being carved in some dusty workshop by a pockmarked man in a leather vest. I saw it being hoisted onto the wall. I saw screaming mobs throwing torches and pulling down sculptures from the cathedral. I saw clouds race overhead, and the sun rise and set, each image passing so quickly in front of me that I couldn't grasp any details. I felt dizzy with all the changes and thought I would puke.

When it was over, I was alone on the gallery, queasy and shuddering. No tourists posing for pictures, no dad, no brother. Just me. And when I looked down at the broad plaza in front of the cathedral, there were no more souvenir hawkers or throngs of schoolkids. Instead men sauntered by in tall black hats, wearing elegant jackets and carrying canes. Women strolled in long skirts, twirling parasols over their shoulders. I blinked and looked again, trying to find the camera crew that must be filming the movie.

That's when I noticed that as far as I could see—which was pretty far—there wasn't a single car, bus, or taxi on the streets. There were horse-drawn carriages, some open, some closed, carts pulled by donkeys, and people walking. And here's the weirdest thing—there was no Eiffel Tower, like it had been plucked off the landscape.

I was still in Paris. The question was when?

July 2?

I wrote the date but I really had no idea what day or year or century it was. Just from the clothes I was wearing—no jeans or T-shirt, but a dark green dress with a tight waist and high, choky neck—I knew I wasn't in the twenty-first century, or even the twentieth. No cars, no airplanes, no TV antennas. No Dad or Malcolm either. But I was still holding my sketchbook. That's the only thing that was the same.

I touched the gargoyle again, but nothing happened. I touched all the gargoyles in a sweaty panic. No luck. I was still wearing a weird dress, and the Eiffel Tower was still gone. I wish I could say that I was brave and resourceful and figured out exactly what strange supernatural glitch had hurled me back in time. But I wasn't. I was knee-shaking, stomach-clenching scared.

"Okay," I told myself. "You're alive and not hurt, so stay calm." I took a deep breath and plunged back down the winding, dark staircase, holding up the annoying skirt to keep from tripping on it until I flung myself out into the glaringly sunny street.

And bumped right into someone.

"So sorry," I babbled. "I couldn't see."

The boy looked about my age, and that made him seem friendly. Even more friendly when he asked, "You are American?"

"Yes! And you speak English!"

"Some. The artist I work for likes to practice English and he helps me. His good friend is American and she helps me also. So with them both, I have two helps. Allow me to introduce myself. I am called Claude."

Claude was a terrible name for him because he wasn't cloddish at all. He was lean and muscular, with deep brown eyes, hair so black it had a blue sheen, and a lopsided smile. Maybe it was the cute French accent that went with the cute French face, or the adorable way he said "two helps." Whatever it was, I felt I could trust him.

"Nice to meet you, Claude. I'm Mira." Actually, this much I could say in French, but since he was speaking

English, it seemed easier to stick with the language I knew best. "I know this sounds odd, but could you tell me what day it is?"

"Today is Tuesday."

"I mean the date. And the year." I hoped I didn't sound crazy.

"The second of April, 1881," he said as if I'd simply asked the time.

Now I really thought I would throw up! What was I doing in 1881? How did I get here?

"Mademoiselle." Claude took my elbow, supporting my suddenly jelly-filled legs. "You don't look well. If you like, I will accompany you to your hotel."

I didn't know where to go or what to do. Did my hotel even exist in 1881? I mumbled the address.

"Place Sainte-Catherine?" Claude arched an eyebrow. "You are Jewish?"

Who says that? I wondered. The only time anybody asked me about my religion was when teachers wanted to know why I was absent on Rosh Hashana or Yom Kippur.

"I do not mean to pry. It is just that only the Jews live there. Nobody else wants to live with the Jews."

Wow. I'd heard my grandparents tell stories about anti-Semitism, but it all seemed quaint and far away. I guessed in 1881, it wasn't so quaint. I considered saying I was a nice Christian girl. But only for a second.

"Don't worry about walking me to my hotel. I wouldn't want you to dirty yourself with my company." If only he weren't so cute, I could have sounded snarkier. Instead I just sounded mad.

He laughed and took my arm. "It is not a problem."

"Did I miss something? Aren't you worried about being with a Jew?"

"Mademoiselle Mira, I am Jewish. So now it is you who must worry."

I felt like a total idiot. "Open mouth, insert foot."

"What do you say? I do not understand."

"Never mind," I said. "Some things shouldn't be translated. Like my stupidity."

I thought I would know the way back to the hotel but everything looked so different that I would never have found it without Claude. The narrow streets were crowded with carts, some pushed by men, others pulled by horses. A man selling umbrellas walked by, carrying his stock rolled up in a rug. Another man balanced a wooden board with loaves of bread on his head. Small stores sold wine or cheese or books, with barrels of wares set out before the windows. The streets were a strange mix of grubby dirtiness and smooth polish. Kids in rags jostled women in silks in front of elegant apartments alternating with ramshackle, dingy buildings.

We found the address but no hotel. Even if it had been there, my room had been reserved in 2012, not 1881. I pushed down the rising panic, but what was I supposed to do now? I didn't belong here!

I slumped down on a bench in the square, trying not to cry.

"I have a maid's room at the artist's house. We can ask the monsieur if you can stay with me," Claude offered. If he thought I was an idiot for forgetting where my hotel really was, he didn't say. He was too sweet for that.

It was a long walk all the way to the artsy neighborhood of Montmartre. I almost suggested we take the metro, except of course there wasn't one in 1881. We turned off the broad tree-lined boulevard onto small streets that grew narrower, more winding, and steep. Now the houses weren't as grand, and alongside the small shops and homes, there were restaurants with large gardens. We passed vegetable plots, a small vineyard, a yard penning in goats and sheep, even a windmill. It seemed like there was as much farmland as houses, making this part of Paris feel like a country village. It was like I was walking in a painting or some period-piece movie.

Then I saw her—Mom! I swear it was her, only she was wearing 1881 clothes like everyone else. She had her hair tucked into a hat that looked like a puff pastry on her head and was sitting at a sidewalk café with a man sprouting a giant walrusy moustache. He looked like an unbaked biscuit with seeds for eyes.

"Mom!" I yelled, running toward her, stumbling on my

stupid skirt and pointy-toed shoes. If I'd been wearing jeans and sneakers, I would have caught her. If she'd been a normal mother, she would have caught me. Instead she looked at me. And then she bolted.

"Mom!" I screeched, louder and shriller. "Where are you going? Why did you leave?"

But there was no answer. She jumped into a waiting carriage and was gone. Disappearing again, this time right in front of

 my eyes.

"What is she doing here? Do you know?" I bellowed at the walrus man.

"Mira, calm down, please." Claude took my arm. "What is wrong?"

"Just tell me," I glared at Mr. Walrus, shooting all my rage at Mom through my eyes right into his doughy forehead.

"So sorry, mademoiselle! Sit down, please! Have a glass of water! A little calm, please!" The man was babbling, but he spoke good English.

"How do you know my mother?"

"She is a friend, nothing more. We have certain interests in common, that is all." Mr. Walrus dabbed at his sweaty face with his handkerchief. "She told me that I might see you and

I should say how sorry she is not to be with you. And she gave me this. For you." He thrust out a pale blue envelope.

"She knew I'd be here?" Which was stranger—that she expected me or that she was in 1881 Paris herself? Had she sent the postcard from this time? How could that be? I remembered the stamp looked old and so did the card, but I hadn't noticed the postmark. And why leave a letter for me instead of talking to me herself? It all smelled fishy.

"What exactly are your interests?" I asked, snatching the letter.

"I sadly cannot inform you of this. That is for your admirable mother."

The man stood up, tipped his hat as if we'd had an ordinary polite chat, and waddled away like a demented penguin. I just stood there hating him. And crying like an idiot.

"Mira, please, explain me what is wrong."

There was way too much to tell. So all I said was, "Let's go to your place."

I guess he was trying to distract me because while we walked, Claude kept up a constant chatter. He told me about his work, running errands for the painter, a man who lived alone except for Claude and the housekeeper. He told me about all the important people who came to the studio—writers, journalists, artists. He said a lot of names, and at first I didn't pay attention to them. I was thinking about Mom and the letter I was too scared to open.

Then Claude listed names I knew, names everyone knows. Cézanne, Renoir, Gauguin, Mary Cassatt, really famous paint-ers. I started paying attention.

"Who is this artist you work for?" I asked.

"Monsieur Degas. He is a genius."

Degas? I had a print of one of his paintings, *The Dancing Lesson*, in my room. Mom had taken me to the big Impressionist exhibit in San Francisco last year. If I knew what was going on, I could be excited about this time-travel thing. But I was too scared and too angry. The only thing that kept me calm was the warmth of Claude's arm linked in mine.

Claude opened the door to a small two-story house, leading me into a room full of chairs, a sofa, and, most of all, paintings. Small sculptures of horses and women were scattered on shelves, tables, and chairs, some in clay, others in plas-ter or bronze. There was something raw about these figures. You could see the marks of fingers pressing into the clay but instead of looking clumsy, the handling gave the pieces an incredible energy, an urgency. One horse looked like it would leap off its base and gallop around the room. A woman in a tub twisted to scrub her back, and I could swear she moved, she seemed so alive.

All over the walls were pictures that in the future would be in museums. Some I could tell were by Degas, ballet dancers like my poster, women bathing or trying on hats. But a lot of them weren't. If I'd taken that art history class Mom wanted me to, I'm sure I could have named the artists. The only one I knew for sure was Van Gogh. No one has such thick, globby brushstrokes, such strange greens and yellows as Van Gogh.

Besides the paintings, Japanese prints were tacked onto the walls, and piles of books teetered on the floor and on shelves. It was all a mess, but the most artistic mess I'd ever seen.

"Sit." Claude steered me into a chair next to a small statuette of a rearing horse. "I will ask the housekeeper to make us some tea."

The letter was smoldering in my fingers. Even with so much to look at in the room, I couldn't wait any longer. As soon as Claude left, I tore open the flap and pulled out the single page.

Dearest Mira,

If you're reading this, it's because you've inherited the gift of time travel. And you know that I'm here in nineteenth-century Paris. That's why I'm not home in Berkeley, but as soon as I can find a way to return, I will.

I wish I could tell you how to control the gift, but all I can say is that you need a touchstone. The details are different for each of us, so you must discover for yourself how to move between the centuries.

The rules I can tell you are these:

No one can know you're from the future, or you'll be stuck in whatever time period you're in.

You can't bring anyone or anything back with you.

People from the same family should not time-travel together since that doubles the chances of changing their descendants' lives. It's too dangerous to risk. That's one reason why I'm telling you all this in a letter and not in person.

Once we're both home, we can talk about all this. For now, please know that I love you, Malcolm, and Dad. I would never have left if the reasons weren't so absolutely urgent. Trust me to find my way back to you as soon as I can.

Love,
Mom

The letter raised more questions than it answered. Why had she traveled to Paris, 1881, in the first place? Why didn't she tell us she *could* time-travel, that I might be able to too? What about Malcolm? Dad? Were they here some-where and I needed to find them? And what was a touchstone? How was I supposed to figure out where one was and how to use it?

Dearest Mira,

If you're reading this, it's because you're inherited the gift of time travel. And you know that I'm here, in 19th century Paris. That's why I'm not home, but as soon as I can find a way to return, I will.

I wish I could tell you how to control the gift, but all I can say is that you need a Touchstone. The details are different for each of us, so you must discover for yourself how to move between the centuries.

The rules I can tell you are these:

No one can know you're from the future or you'll be stuck in whatever time period you're in. You can't bring anyone or anything back with you. People from the same family should not time travel together since that doubles the chances of changing their descendants' lives. It's too dangerous to risk. That's one reason why I'm telling you all this in a letter.

Once we're both home, we can talk about all this. For now, please trust that I'm doing the right thing. I love you all and never would have left if the reasons weren't so absolutely urgent.

I'll be home as soon as possible!

love, Mom

I read the letter through a second time, searching for answers in what she didn't say, but this time all I noticed was the rule about people who are related not travel-ing together. I didn't get how stopping to talk to me would change anyone's future. What was so risky about that?

Stupid rules, with no useful information at all. But I had to admit, I was relieved. She hadn't cheated on Dad. She hadn't run away from us. She was stuck in another century. With me, which meant I wasn't alone here. And I would be able to get home somehow. I just had to find a touchstone, whatever that was.

There was something else about the letter that gave me a hint of satisfaction, even as I worried about how I'd ever get home. Mom said I'd inherited her ability to time-travel. So maybe I wasn't pretty, smart, or artistic, but I had something from her.

Now here I was in a house full of great art, about to meet one of the most famous painters of all time. It seemed ironic that the gift I'd actually gotten from Mom showed me how much I hadn't inherited the artistic talent I'd always secretly wanted. Looking at the pictures around me, I knew I'd never come even close.

Claude came back with a clattering of cups on a tray. I folded the letter up and stuck it in my sketchbook. I didn't have a pocket, a purse, a backpack. What else was I supposed to do?

"Why were you so angry with that man and woman? And what means 'mom'?" Claude handed me a teacup with a gilt filigreed handle.

"Mom, you know, that's English for thief, pickpocket," I lied. "She stole my purse when I was on the train. Which is why I have no money." The excuse just popped into my head and Claude seemed to believe it. I wished I could forget about Mom, forget about the letter, and just enjoy being with him. I liked the way he looked at me, like he was really paying attention, like he cared what I said. But I couldn't shake off how angry I was. And under the rage was a sharp sliver of fear. What was I doing here?

I was saved from any more awkward explanations by Monsieur Degas. He was tall, thin, and stoop-shouldered, with a long nose and full lips. But what I noticed most were his eyes. They looked right into you like they saw into your soul. But in a nice way, as if you were sharing a joke.

"Claude," he said. "*Veux-tu faire la présentation?*"

"I beg pardon, monsieur. This is Mademoiselle Mira. She is American and in need of a place to lodge. I thought perhaps she could stay here. Mira, this is the eminent painter, Monsieur Degas."

Claude had stood up, so I did too. I was so nervous that my cheeks were hot and pink. "I'm honored to meet you, monsieur," I said, not sure if I should offer my hand to shake or curtsey or bow or who knows what.

"The honor is all mine." Degas dipped his head in a short bow and gestured for me to sit again. He folded himself up into a chair, looking far too tall and angular for its roundness, stroking his chin with his elegant fingers. I have this thing about hands. Some are stubby and thick; other people have flat, shovelly fingers, and then there are hands like Degas's. His were supple and intelligent. I could imagine them shaping the sculptures all around us.

"How is it that you speak English so well?" I asked, ashamed of my few words of French.

"I have family in your New Orleans, and I have spent many happy months visiting them. I must say I love the English language! I am enchanted to have the occasion to practice it with you. Do you know my favorite phrase at the moment? Turkey buzzard! Such a marvelous sound! Do you know them, the turkey buzzard?"

I was talking to a famous artist about turkey buzzards?

"I have seen them, but it is not the bird itself which interests me," Degas continued. "They are rather ugly, you know. But what a word—turkey! And buzzard! And then, you have the two together—turkey buzzard!"

"And what do you call them in French?" I asked.

"Turkey buzzard!" laughed Degas. "Because they do not exist here, so we have no name for them. Like that other creature that is so distinctly American, the one with the white stripe on its back and the foul smell when it is fearful."

"A skunk?"

"Yes, a skunk! Now that is another marvelous word. Skunk!"

And the way he said it, it was. Degas was funny and gentle and curious about me. I didn't have to worry about what to say because he asked me questions and all I had to do was answer.

For some reason I'd always thought he was an old crank who painted beautiful pictures, a lonely old bachelor who hated people. But from the way he talked, he had loads of friends and went out almost every night—to the opera, the ballet, the symphony, gallery exhibitions, dinner with friends. I liked him not just as an artist, but as a person. He was so easy to talk to that I almost told him the truth about who I was and where—I mean, when—I really belonged.

But I remembered Rule Number One and said I was supposed to be with my aunt, only she'd been called away to visit a sick friend in Italy. There was no room for me to go with her and I really wanted to see Paris, so my aunt was supposed to arrange for my hotel and I'd wait for her here. Only it seemed like my aunt had forgotten and there was no hotel. Normally I'm a terrible liar, but after the Mom-equals-pickpocket story, I felt more inventive. Degas and Claude both swallowed my story.

"Claude thought maybe I could stay here," I said hopefully.

Degas shook his head. "Much as I would love to have you as a guest, it is not proper for a young lady who is no relation to stay with two such bachelors as ourselves. It would be better for you to rest with my good friend, Mary Cassatt. She is American like you and has a tender heart. I am sure she would welcome a fellow countryman. See that painting over there, the one of the girl combing her hair? That is her work. Charming, no?"

I thought the girl's neck was too long and the pose was awkward, but maybe that was what Degas meant by charming. Like the word "interesting," which basically means "I don't like it but don't want to hurt anybody's feelings."

Anyway the important thing was whether I could stay with her, not admire her painting. So I smiled and nodded and took a sip of my tea, trying to behave the way a young lady should in 1881. My version, that is.

I guess I was lucky that if I had to go back in time, I ended up in Paris on the opening day of the sixth exhibit of the Impressionist painters. Except I wasn't supposed to say "Impressionist" or "Impressionism" because Degas hated those words. Critics called the pictures that because they showed a specific moment in time, a fleeting impression, rather than the stiff, classical paintings of mythological subjects that had been the standard before. But Degas hated the term, which came from a picture of a sunrise by Monet called—you guessed it— *Impression: Sunrise.*

He considered their painting "realism," and he detested Monet. Which was probably why there weren't any paintings by him in the show. Claude said there were plenty by Degas, Cassatt, and Gauguin. I wondered if those artists were at the exhibit, if I'd get to meet Gauguin. I'd heard of him. He painted pictures of people in Tahiti in bright colors with bold outlines.

Not like Degas at all, almost the opposite in fact, but still striking and beautiful.

Before we left for the exhibit, while I was waiting for Degas and Claude to change into evening clothes (whatever those were), I walked around the studio, wishing I could magically change my own sweaty dress into a proper gown. But when I saw a sculpture of a dancer, I didn't care what I was wearing, where Mom was, or how I had gotten here. All I could think about was this absolutely perfect figure, so different from the abstract metal shapes—all sharp angles and brushed steel— that my grandfather made.

It was a ballet dancer, standing with her hands behind her back, her chin tilted up. The kind of thing you'd see in bronze in a museum. Only it wasn't bronze in 1881. It was wax that had been painted to look like skin and the tutu was real cloth, the hair real hair, the ribbon real ribbon. It was so perfect that you'd swear the girl was breathing. Looking at it, the world seemed whole and perfect. I could feel my lips smiling, my eyes brighten, my body fill with air and light, a gift the statue was giving me.

There was something magical about the figure. I was drawn to it just like the gargoyle and had the sudden urge to touch it. I thought about Mom's letter and wondered if the statue could be a touchstone even though it was wax, not stone. I reached out a cautious finger and delicately touched the toe of her slipper, holding my breath. I closed my eyes, waiting. Nothing. Except when I opened them again, I noticed a small scrap of paper sticking out from under the base. I was super careful to work the paper free without disturbing the statue.

Something was written in cramped handwriting on the narrow strip.

Mira,

I hope you find this because if you do, it means you're on the right track. I realize now that you have a job to do in this time too, just as I do. I can't tell you what, except that it has something to do with intolerance, with fighting against prejudice. I'm sure you'll figure it out for yourself. Just pay attention and do the right thing. Then everything will be okay.

Love,
Mom

A job? The right thing? Pay attention? Why couldn't Mom just tell me what I needed to do?

I crumpled up the paper as the door opened and Claude walked in. He looked handsome in his long black coat, starched white shirt, and black silk tie. I glanced back at the statue, mute in its perfection. I was in Paris with a charming young man, seeing incredible art and meeting famous people. That was something I was happy to pay attention to. Maybe I'd figure out what Mom wanted me to, but in the meantime, I wanted to enjoy myself. If I could stop myself from worrying about how strange this all was.

Claude led me to a carriage waiting outside. Degas was already seated with his elegant top hat resting on his lap. I was embarrassed by my dirty hem, scuffed shoes, and less-than-fresh smell, but Claude's gentle hands on my waist, lifting me into the carriage, made me feel pretty, despite all the grit. And sitting across from Degas, it was like I could breathe in his classy attitude and make it my own.

The gallery was already crowded when we got there. The men all wore black like Degas and Claude, while the women wore a rainbow of colors, blues, violets, pinks, yellows, and greens, with hats punctuating their heads.

"Can you introduce me to people?" I asked Claude.

"Are you tired of me already?" he teased.

"Of course not!"

"But I am not a successful artist with a painting in this show."

"Not yet, but next time, I'm sure," I said. I didn't know whether to take him seriously or not. Was he really upset not to be included? I thought he was studying art, not a painter already. After all, he didn't seem much older than me. "I'd love to see your pictures. I'm sure they're wonderful," I gushed. And immediately felt stupid. I would hate for someone to talk to me that way, as if I was a baby. Why did I always say the wrong thing around him?

Claude winced. I couldn't blame him. I'd never have the courage to show anyone my clumsy drawings. I seemed to keep putting my foot in my mouth around him.

"There is Seurat—and his new picture," he said, changing the subject. "You will like them both, I think."

He took me by the elbow and steered me to a large canvas of people in their Sunday best relaxing on the banks of a river done in dots of color. It was kind of like a pixel print where up close all you saw were blobs of color, but from far away, the blobs or pixels came together into shapes of people, parasols, trees. Standing near it was a young man with thick, dark curly hair, sad, droopy eyes, and a droopy moustache and beard that made him look even sadder.

"Georges-Pierre Seurat," Claude said. "May I introduce my friend, Mademoiselle Mira."

"Enchanted," I said, taking his limp hand. "Your painting is beautiful." I wasn't sure if that was the right word to use. Maybe he wanted to hear "modern, inventive, fresh, original." Maybe "beautiful" was an insult. I cringed, waiting for his response.

"Kind of you to say so," Seurat said. "I am honored to be included in such company." He waved his arm at the other paintings. "I fear the critics will be harsh with my spots of color so I cherish your compliment all the more."

"Ah, Seurat, there you are!" A wolfish-looking man in a top hat stepped between us. "I want you to meet the countess."

I was curious to meet the countess too, but Claude pulled me away. "We are here to see paintings, are we not?"

We wedged between knots of people as the exhibit grew more crowded by the minute. I wondered if people would criticize Seurat's picture as he feared, but all I heard were comments about the lights.

"It is electricity! Can you believe it?" a woman murmured to the stout man at her side.

"How does it work?" wondered another. "What if it stops suddenly? How will we see?"

"The lights were Degas's idea," Claude explained. "Many people do not quite trust these new electric lights, but he wanted people to see the art at night when they are free from working. He insisted that gaslight casts a reddish glow that ruins the colors."

"I can see that he cares about colors! Was it his idea too, to have the gallery painted this way?" The walls were lilac with canary yellow trim, bright blues, and deep reds.

Claude nodded. "I was not sure, but Degas said they would make the colors in the art richer. And now that I see it, he is right."

You would think all that color would clash and make one

big ugly mush, but like Claude said, somehow it all worked. It was way better than the regular boring white, cream, or gray museum walls we have in modern times.

The other thing people talked about was something that wasn't there. In the middle of one of the rooms was an empty glass box on a stand.

"I've heard it's a marvel," a woman with a feathery hat said to the monocled man next to her.

"So why isn't it here?" snapped the man. "Is it finished or not?"

"What's supposed to be there?" I asked Claude.

"That dancer you were looking at in Degas's studio. He says it is not quite done yet."

"I thought it was perfect."

"You have seen it?" asked an Englishman with a pointy orange beard and matching circumflex eyebrows. "I've heard it's absolutely ingenious, more a living, breathing creature than a sculpture."

"It will be on exhibit soon," Claude said. "Maybe even by tomorrow."

There were beautiful paintings by all the big names Degas had mentioned, but the most brilliant thing I saw that evening was the statue back in the studio. Maybe I'd time-traveled just to see that. It was definitely worth paying attention to.

April 3, 1881

As Degas predicted, Mary Cassatt kindly gave me a room and a place where I could speak English and not worry about my poor French at all. She was a small, slender woman with a quick smile and warm, inviting eyes. I felt at home with her right away.

"How do you know Degas?" I asked over croissants and coffee at breakfast that first morning.

"I met him in the Louvre when I was there copying a painting. I was at my lowest, having been refused by the Salon, and he was kind and encouraging." Mary smiled at the memory. "You know, the Salon was the official stamp of approval for any artist, but they only accepted the usual classical subjects. They didn't like pictures of everyday

life, so naturally they rejected my art. Not Degas! And his opinion meant so much more to me than the foolish Salon. He had no idea how much I'd drooled over his pastels when I saw them in gallery windows! Truly, seeing his work changed my life. He was a mentor for me before we even met. His pictures were teaching me. And then in person, well…"

She waved her hand as if summoning up all Degas had done for her.

I drew constantly. I couldn't stop my fingers from grabbing a pen or pencil and trying to capture what I saw. But that didn't make me anything close to a real artist. For a second I wondered if I could become a painter like Mary if only I had the right teacher. Except that it takes more than a brilliant teacher. It takes a talented student.

I wanted to ask about Claude but didn't dare. Where was his family? How long had he worked for Degas? And, most importantly, did he have a girlfriend? Instead I said, "Do you ever miss America?"

Mary laughed. "Not at all! I missed my family, but my parents and sister moved close by, so that's home enough for me. I could never be an artist in America. Women simply aren't allowed."

I thought about that, what America would be like in the 1880s. Good thing I was born when I was. If I ever got to live in the twenty-first century again. I felt a sharp pang of homesickness and stuffed it deep down. I couldn't allow myself to panic. I was safe and being taken care of and should feel grateful for that while I figured out what to do next.

I reminded myself I was lucky to be with Mary and even more lucky to have found Claude as a friend. Except I wanted him to be more than a friend. That evening, we walked along the Seine, admiring the sunset. The city was so beautiful and his eyes so warm, and it was all so romantic. I leaned into his chest, tilted my lips up to his, and waited.

Nothing.

Wasn't he supposed to kiss me? I couldn't be the one to kiss him. That would be, I don't know, pushy, awkward, and just plain wrong. Everyone knows the guy is supposed to pull the girl in close, lean down, and give her a soulful, tender kiss. Especially in the nineteenth century.

Everyone except Claude knew that. He cleared his throat and turned bright red and pulled away from me. Not toward, but away, completely backward.

Then he started babbling about how fond Degas was of me, how he appreciated my wit (wit?), my keen eye, my delightful Americanisms. Nothing as charming as "turkey buzzard," but close.

"In fact, he was amazed when I told him you're Jewish," Claude said, totally ruining the romantic mood.

"Why would you tell him that? Who cares whether I'm Jewish or not?"

"He does, of course! Monsieur Degas is a brilliant artist, a kind gentleman, but that hardly makes him a friend of the Jews. He's quite opinionated about it really, though he laughs and says some of his best friends are Jewish. Like me. And now you."

Instead of being kissed, I was stuck in a ridiculous conversation. "I don't want to be a token Jewish friend," I snapped. But I liked Degas. He seemed so modern in so much of his thinking—like having faith in electricity, respecting women artists, valuing people like laundresses who did hard drudgery and painting their pictures. Yet he was old-fashioned enough to share that most ancient of prejudices, anti-Semitism. I didn't know how to make all those things fit in the same person.

I thought of Mary Cassatt and how much she admired Degas. And Claude, who was Jewish himself, worshipped him. Did that mean I could still like him? I wasn't sure what I felt anymore.

I hurried across the bridge facing Notre Dame. The square in front of the cathedral was full of people out for a stroll, and I bet I could find somebody there who wouldn't ask if I was Jewish. Maybe even somebody who'd want to kiss me. That would show Claude.

"Mira! I am desolate. I did not mean to do bad to you!"

I could hear him behind me, but I wasn't looking back and

I wasn't waiting for him either. I needed to be alone to sort out what I was feeling. Maybe I wanted him to follow me, but I wasn't sure even of that.

I threaded my way through clusters of skirts and trousers, until a pair of stout gray legs under a round belly caught my eye. Something about the man's rolling gait was familiar. It was the walrus-moustache man, the one I'd seen with Mom! Maybe this was what Mom meant by paying attention.

He was walking toward the cathedral, and he kept looking nervously over his shoulder as if he expected to see someone. Mom, maybe? I ducked behind a woman in a wide yellow skirt, then behind the cart of a man selling paper cones of nuts. The Walrus Man zigzagged across the square before darting into one of the side doors.

I followed him inside, being careful that he couldn't see me. That's when I noticed I wasn't the only one following him. A beautiful woman with thick dark hair pinned up under a black velvet hat, flashing violet eyes, and stunningly chiseled features was carefully staying several paces behind Mr. Walrus, ducking behind columns the same way I'd hidden in the square. Maybe she was the person he'd been looking for. She certainly looked like someone a man would want to find, though she clearly didn't want to be seen.

I followed her following him. It would have been funny except it was all so dead serious. When Mr. Walrus slipped into a side chapel, the woman sat in a pew in the last row. I slid behind a column, spying on both of them.

Mr. Walrus looked around. The woman pulled her shawl over her bowed head and murmured as if she was praying. Her act must have convinced Mr. Walrus because he turned to the side altar and slipped something under the flowers there. Then he reached out and touched the statue of Mary over the altar.

There wasn't a bolt of light or a clap of thunder. Just a buzz of static, wavy air, and then where he'd been, there was nothing.

I thought the woman would freak, but she didn't. She scowled, her perfect face blackening with a scary flash of anger. Before she could do anything, I dashed in front of her and snatched what Mr. Walrus had hidden on the altar. Like what I'd found under Degas's dancer, it was a narrow slip of paper. I gripped it tight in my sweaty hand and turned to go.

"Not so fast!" the woman hissed in English. "Give it to me, or I'll break your arm." She grabbed my wrist and twisted it behind my back, hard. "You have no idea what you're doing. If you did, you'd give me that paper."

I tried to bite her, scratch her with my free arm. "Let me go!" I yelled as loud as I could.

"You fool!" the woman whispered, wrenching my arm so hard I thought it would break.

"*Help!*" I screamed. "A thief! Stop the thief!"

"*Arrêt!*" yelled a man, running toward us.

"They'll think you're the thief, in your dingy dress, you idiot!" she spat. "Because you are! You're the thief!" With a final twist, the woman threw me onto the hard stone floor and forced open my fingers, snatching the note. "Go home!" she commanded. "You don't belong here. It's wrong, completely wrong!" She rushed off, leaving me panting on the ground.

"Are you all right, miss?" a monk asked in French, helping me up. Another man offered me his handkerchief, and a woman ran to fetch some water. They were all so kind, but I wasn't fine, not at all. I'd let that witch have the note. I unclasped my fingers, licking my palm where the nails had dug in so deeply I'd drawn blood. There was still a scrap of paper there, a corner of the note. All I could see was "Serena, you need…"

The note was to Mom.

The bad news was that the woman had the note. The good news was that Mom would be coming here to pick it up. I'd get to talk to her at last.

So I thanked my rescuers, drank the water, wiped the tears from my face, and sat back down in the chapel. Just like I'd seen the beautiful but nasty woman do, I pulled my shawl over my head like I was a little old lady praying. And waited.

I sat so long that the chill from the stones around me seeped into my bones. Now I was shivering from the cold as well as fear, and Mom still hadn't come. She would never come. Stupid me, to think I could save her from anything. I wrapped my shawl tighter around my shoulders and got up to leave.

And that was when Mom walked in.

"Mom!" I gasped, the shawl dropping to the floor.

This is the part when a normal mother would run to her daughter, hug her, and tell her everything would be okay. Instead Mom looked panicked, terrified really. She shook her head sadly and ran out the heavy front door.

I rushed after her, but sure enough, she'd disappeared again in the darkening crowds of people rushing home to dinner. Was this because of the rule about family members not time-traveling together? That still didn't make sense to me. Or did she know what had happened with the Walrus man, that the beautiful but scary woman had her note? Was Mom in trouble?

I wanted to be mad at her, but instead I was scared. And confused. How was paying attention going to answer all the questions I had?

April 5, 1881

I still hadn't kissed Claude. Or I should say, he hadn't kissed me. I still hadn't found Mom. I still didn't know what job I was supposed to do or why Mom was so scared.

What I had done was gotten to know Mary Cassatt and Degas a lot better. Yesterday when I was at Degas's with Mary, a painter named Renoir came by with some sketches he wanted to show his friends. He was a small man with quick, bird-like motions and round dark eyes. I thought since his art was soft and sweet, he would be too, but he was nervous and fidgety, laughing in sharp barks, talking so fast I could barely under-stand him, even when he spoke English.

"I am thinking of traveling to Algeria, Degas. You should come with me. Think of the colors we'd see."

"Algeria?" asked Mary. "Why Algeria?"

"I bet I can guess," said Degas. "You want to paint the same kind of brilliant watercolors Delacroix did."

Renoir yipped a short laugh. "Exactly! I fear painting in Paris is turning my colors to sugar. It's all too sweet here. I need the glaring southern light, the dark-skinned Algerian beauties instead of all these creamy pale French women."

"In your hands, it'll all turn to pastry," Degas said. "You can't help yourself."

"Mary, you come with me then, since Edgar will not."

"I'm tempted," Mary said. "But since my sister isn't well, I don't want to go far."

"What is wrong with your sister?" I asked, then immediately felt I'd been rude. "I mean, if you don't mind saying."

"No, no, it's kind of you to ask. She has a weak constitution and always seems to be sick with something. Nothing serious, though, I'm sure."

"You must make sure she stays warm," said Degas, leaning forward to take Mary's hand. "The Paris chill can creep into your bones. Perhaps you should take her to sunny Algeria with Renoir."

"Yes!" crowed Renoir. "That will make us all happy—me, you, and your dear sister."

"I wish I could go!" I blurted out. Why did I keep saying things I regretted?

"You are welcome too, of course," said Renoir. He hadn't paid much attention to me before but now he beamed at me. "Perhaps I could paint you. You have a dark, olive skin, almost Algerian. You would make a splendid model!"

I could feel my checks turn hot and red. Posing for an artist, even a famous one like Renoir, sounded totally embarrassing. Besides, I wanted to do the drawing, not be drawn.

"Don't tease her like that, Renoir," Mary chided. "You're tormenting the poor child. Come, Mira, I think it's time for us to go. And not to Algeria."

Besides Renoir, I've met ballet dancers, café singers, and one of Degas's closest friends, Ludovic Halévy. Who is Jewish! That meant Degas didn't think of me as a token Jewish friend, and he couldn't be that anti-Semitic. Degas had known Halévy since they went to school together, and he ate dinner with the whole family once or twice a week.

He doted on their children and stayed at their country homes, and Halévy's wife developed his photographs. (Degas is really into the new art of photography. I couldn't help thinking how much Dad would love to meet him.) Degas had many friends, but nobody was as close to him as the Halévys. Mom's note had said to keep an eye out for intolerance so I was relieved that I didn't have to think of Degas as prejudiced

against Jews anymore. I could just enjoy him as a friend.

Today we went to the races. Degas sketched the horses; Claude sketched the crowds; and I sketched it all—horses, people, Degas, and Claude. Mary Cassatt loaned me a parasol and dress since I only had one, and I felt elegant with my hair pinned up and white silk gloves making my fingers look tapered and slender.

"Don't move. Stay just as you are," Claude said.

"You're drawing me?" My cheeks flamed.

"You're the most lovely thing here. How can I resist?"

I lowered my eyes. If that was true, why hadn't he kissed me yet? I'd given him so many chances.

"Are you an artist now?" I asked instead. "Not just an artist's assistant?"

"I am trying to be an artist," Claude corrected. "Which is why I am an artist's assistant. Who better to learn from than Degas? And I saw you sketching yourself, so you too, are an artist."

"No," I said. "I was taking notes, that's all. Things that pop into my head. It's kind of a hobby, I guess." I gripped my sketchbook tightly.

His fingers moved quickly over the paper. The rasp of chalk on paper, horses snorting, hooves drumming on the dirt track, people murmuring and cheering—I let the sounds wash over me, along with the lemony sunlight and the grassy breezes. It was a perfect moment. Time could stop right now, I thought, and I'd be happy like this.

But of course time doesn't stop. It moves, backward I suppose as well as forward, but it moves. I began to wonder if Mom was still in this time and place. And if she was, what was she doing here? More importantly, what was I doing here? And when would we both go home? Paris was beautiful, but I missed Dad and Malcolm. And as nice as everyone was to me, I didn't belong here. I wanted to click my heels together like Dorothy in *The Wizard of Oz* and magic my way home again.

I could feel tears of homesickness prick my eyes—and that's when I saw her, with my vision blurred by tears. It was Mom, there in front of me for real! I wanted to rush up and hug her, hold her tight so she couldn't get away, but I was afraid she'd run away again. Maybe if I came up slowly and quietly, the way you try to get close to a wild animal?

I stood watching her, trying to figure out what to do. She walked alongside the track in a melon-colored dress, her arm linked with that of another woman wearing lilac. A man in a military uniform stood at the lilac woman's side, the three of them forming a tight group. They were too far away for me to tell much, except that Mom was talking and the man was leaning toward her, listening intently, while the lilac woman looked horrified by whatever Mom was saying.

Scarier was the woman I saw behind them. It was the beautiful creepy woman, the witch from Notre Dame. She looked ready to claw out Mom's eyes. Now I had no choice but to go to Mom, no matter what the rules said.

"I'm sorry, Claude," I said. "I'll pose for you later." I gathered up my skirts, trying to stride quickly toward Mom. When she saw me, she shook her head, her eyes warning me off.

That didn't stop me. "Excuse me, madame," I said. "You should be careful. There are pickpockets all around, and I recognize a particularly nasty one behind you."

Mom turned pale and nodded. Glancing back at the dark-haired woman, she hurried away with the couple. I lunged toward the woman, not sure if I should trip her or try to throw her to the ground like a football tackle. I just knew I had to stop her.

I snapped my parasol shut, thinking I could use it as a weapon somehow. What I really wanted was some holy water. I should have taken some from the font at the front of Notre Dame. I imagined tossing the water on the beautiful nasty woman and watching her melt into the ground like the Wicked Witch of the West.

"There you are!" she barked, grabbing my wrist with that iron grip of hers. "You naughty girl! I didn't say you could have today off."

"I'm not your maid!" I tried to wrench free but I swear her hands were like the talons of an eagle.

"You're coming home where you belong!" she seethed. Her eyes drilled into me. I didn't know someone so beautiful could be so ugly.

"Get away, you crazy old bag!" I whacked her with the parasol, hitting as hard as I could.

Claude rushed up. Even if he thought I was crazy for beating on an elegant lady, I had to give him credit. He took my side right away. He pulled the woman off me, trying to be a gentleman at the same time.

"Madame has made a mistake, it seems. This young lady is not your servant, and you will leave her in peace." It wasn't a question.

The dark woman glared. She must have been used to men fawning over her, so why wasn't Claude? Then she smiled and her face was serenely beautiful again. "Ah, a mistake. Must be a trick of the light. No harm done, I'm sure."

"Don't try it again," I said. "Ever!"

The woman sniffed and turned away, melting into the crowd. At least I'd kept her away from Mom.

"Mira, she made a simple mistake. Did you have to hit her?"

"She didn't give me much choice." I showed him my wrist where her claw-hand had left deep red marks.

He looked startled, then sad. He lifted my wrist to his face and kissed all along the welts.

A kiss! At last! And even if it wasn't the kind of kiss I'd imagined, I could feel it all the way to my toes.

I didn't know what to say. I didn't want to break the magic spell.

Degas did that. "You two!" he called out. "Why are you dawdling? The light is changing. The air is turning chill. It is time to go home to a nice warm fire."

April 6, 1881

I had seen Mom again, which was good, but I'd also seen the beautiful scary woman, which was bad. Worst of all, I still didn't know what the job was that I was supposed to do and why Mom was here in the first place. I wasn't sure what I was looking for, but I wandered through the streets, searching for some kind of clue, keeping my eyes open like Mom had said. Since Mr. Walrus had left the note for her at Notre Dame, that seemed a good place to try.

By the time I got to the park behind Notre Dame, I was exhausted. I sank down onto a bench by the fountain and looked at the statues climbing the roof of the cathedral, their silhouettes black against the pale blue sky. They were an odd sight, statues where you least expected them. Just like me. I was someplace I didn't belong at all. A place and a time where I would never fit in. I knew there was a reason for the sculptures, probably a kind of prayer reaching up to heaven. But what was the reason for me to be here?

My feet ached. I slipped off my shoes, and the breeze felt so good playing on my toes that I almost didn't notice it. Wedged into the side of my shoe was a folded-up piece of paper.

"That's strange," I thought. "I didn't put that there. Did Mary? Why?" I'd walked so much the creases were worn through, but when I unfolded the paper, I could see it was a letter. From Mom.

Dear Mira,

I need you to understand that I'm here for a very impor-tant reason. Something terrible will happen in the future, in your future, if I can't change things. Time is always splitting off, like binary trees. When it hits a certain bump or hiccup, it splits and then it can go one of two ways.

Our job, mine and now yours, is to make sure the second way heals or prevents the first way. I didn't know you had the gift too, or I would have told you all this in person at home. I'm guessing this is the first time you've time-traveled, which means you're here for a reason. There's something you need to do.

People like us, those who can time-travel, have a heavy responsibility. When something horrendous happens, we're sent into the past to prevent it from happening. Some horrors are too big for us to change, but others can be altered.

There are other time travelers, like the woman at the racetrack, who try to stop us. They're evil people who profit from misery and destruction. We can't let them win.

Since you're here, it means you need to change things too. It all has to do with Dreyfus, the man I was with at the races. I think you are meant to make Degas support him. He's an important public figure and his voice defending Dreyfus could make the difference. You need to make that difference happen. Then find your touchstone and go home. I'm also working to change things, so don't worry about me. You work on Degas. I'll work on Zola.

Love,
Mom

Unlike the other letters, this one actually told me something, but the tone was so tight and worried that it scared me. The something Mom needed to change must be really horrible. And

Dear Mira,

I need you to understand that I'm here for a very important reason. Something terrible will happen in your future if I can't change things. Time is always splitting off, like binary trees. When it comes to a bump or hiccup, it splits and then it can go one of two ways.

Our job, mine and now yours, is to make sure the second way heals or prevents the first. I didn't know you had the gift too or I would have told you all this in person. I'm guessing this is the first time you've time traveled, which means you're here for a reason. There's something you need to do.

People like us, those who can time travel, have a heavy responsibility. When something horrendous will happen, we've sent into the past to prevent it from happening. Some horrors are too big for us to change, but others can be altered.

There are other time travelers, like the women at the races, who try to stop us. They're evil people who profit from misery and destruction. We can't let them win.

Since you're here, it means you need to change things too. It all has to do with Dreyfus, the man I was with at the races. I think you're meant to make Degas feel more warmly toward the Jews. He's an important public figure and his voice defending Dreyfus could make a difference. Make that difference happen, then find your touchstone and go home. I'm also working to change things, through another man, Zola. I'll be home as soon as I can.

Love, Mom

the fact that the beautiful creepy woman was so determined to stop Mom made it even riskier. I wanted to help Mom, like she asked, but now that I knew what my job was, it made no sense. Who was Dreyfus and why did Degas need to support him?

I read the letter again, hoping for more answers, more clarity, but I was just more confused. Except that one thing was clear. I was here for a very specific reason. This wasn't an accident at all. I wondered if that meant I wouldn't find my touchstone until I'd done whatever it was I was supposed to do. Would I be stuck here forever if I couldn't figure it out?

"Excuse me, mademoiselle." A man sat next to me on the bench, far too close for a stranger. I quickly folded up the letter and glared at him. Only it wasn't a stranger—it was the Walrus Man. I thought he'd gone to another time when he vanished in Notre Dame, but here he was, back again.

"I'm Morton, a friend of your mother's," he said, leaning in and speaking in a hoarse whisper. "A time traveler, like yourself. She asked me to find you."

"Is she okay?" I asked. "Where is she?"

"She's fine, she's fine." He wiped beads of sweat off his pasty forehead. "She wants you to go to 1894. That's when you'll be useful to her."

As if I could just open the door that said "1894" and walk through it! How was I supposed to time-travel? I hadn't done any of this on purpose.

Besides, I already had instructions from Mom in her letter. I didn't trust this so-called friend at all. "My mom said I need to get Degas to support Dreyfus," I told him. "So that's what I'll do. Once I figure out who Dreyfus is and why Degas should support him."

"No, that's a waste of time. I told her that would never work. She thinks instead you can save Dreyfus from being accused of treason in the first place. Then Degas's opinion won't matter."

"Why should I believe you?"

"You saw your mother with me. You know she's my friend." He looked surprised that I'd doubt him, which made me believe him even less.

"Being together doesn't make you friends." Everything he said made him even more suspicious.

"I can't prove anything, it's true. And if you don't want to believe me, well, all I can say is that I tried." He shrugged and actually looked relieved. "Maybe it's best if you don't listen to me."

"Even if I wanted to believe you, I don't know how to get to

1894. I don't know how to control time travel. Can you explain it to me?" I didn't trust pasty, sweaty Morton, but I might learn something useful from him.

"I can't tell you how to time-travel. You have to figure that out for yourself, but you need to be looking for something, really looking, to go anywhere. After a while, you develop an instinct for what works." Morton leaned back, looking almost relaxed. "These kinds of things I can tell you, it's allowed, but you'll still have to figure out what works yourself. Anything can be a touchstone. You just have to look. But you should know that sometimes they work only once. You can't always go back and use the same touchstone again."

"What do you mean 'it's allowed'? What isn't allowed?" I asked.

The man turned purply red so suddenly that I thought he was having a heart attack.

"I can't tell you more," he choked. "That's for your mother to do. She said she'd given you the rules."

"She did. She said we shouldn't be in the same time and place since we're related. Is that true?"

The man nodded, his skin blotching into a mottled pink and white as he calmed down. "Better you avoid each other. It's safer for everyone that way. And you know you can't tell anyone you're from the future."

"That's a pretty obvious rule," I said. "More like common

sense. Explain to me about Dreyfus. Why does it matter if he's accused of treason? Why does Mom care?"

"I can tell you what she thinks," the man said. "I don't completely agree with her, you understand, but she's right about this. A single person's life can make an enormous difference."

"So?" I pressed. "Why this man? Who is Dreyfus anyway?"

"He's a captain in the French Army who will be accused of selling military secrets to the Germans."

"Why does Mom care about a traitor?"

"He's accused," snapped Morton. "That doesn't mean he's guilty."

"He must have done something suspicious," I insisted.

"What makes him seem suspicious is that he isn't Christian."

And suddenly it all made sense. Claude's comments about the Jews, Degas's friendship with the Halévys. Dreyfus must be Jewish, and that made him seem automatically guilty.

"I get it," I said. "So Degas needs to like Jews to support Dreyfus?" It kind of made sense, though it seemed stupid to accuse or not accuse, support or not support simply because of somebody's religion.

"Because of how the French military treat Dreyfus, because of their prejudice, the government will collapse and the military will never recover. The direction of France, of all Europe, will be changed. Intolerance will breed more intolerance, which will breed violence. All because of how this one man is unjustly accused." Morton cleared his throat. "That's your mother's opinion, not mine."

"So how does she know what has to be changed? What will turn history down a different path?"

"She doesn't. None of us do. We guess, we try, and we try again." Morton's voice got lower and lower, turning into a whisper. "But it's dangerous. You might think you're doing the right thing and do completely the wrong thing."

"And what about the people who try to stop you? Like the woman who followed you into Notre Dame? How dangerous is she?"

"What woman?" Morton looked terrified. "Describe her!"

I told him what she looked like and what had happened after he vanished that day in the cathedral. I was going to add the scene from the racetrack, but he interrupted me, wringing his sausage fingers together in worry.

"This is dreadful, just dreadful! She knows what Serena is doing. She knows what you're doing. Maybe it's best to forget about all this. Yes, just forget about it. Don't try to do anything! Find a touchstone and go home!"

"But then she wins! Mom said we have to do this—it's really important. She said this affects my future, so it's not a vague problem but something very specific. Besides, we can't let the bad guys win." I was surprised Morton would give up so easily. Could I really trust this man?

"She told you that!" Mr. Walrus squealed in panic. "She shouldn't have!"

"Why? What is she really trying to stop?" I pressed.

"This, the whole Dreyfus mess," he insisted. "Which will lead to the collapse of the French government and to some other issues that are all connected. Maybe something that happens in your future, but I don't know anything about that. And you shouldn't either!"

Obviously he knew a lot more than he was admitting. "What about that woman? Who is she exactly?"

"Someone you should avoid at all costs!" Morton snapped. "Stay far, far away from her!"

"But who is she?"

"I can't tell you any more. I really can't," he said. He looked scared and miserable at the same time.

"Can you at least tell me what happens in 1894?" I asked. "What am I supposed to do?"

"You can stop Dreyfus from ever being accused. A French spy, working in the German Embassy as a cleaning woman, will find a torn-up note that lists military information passed to the German military attaché. That's the note Dreyfus will be accused of writing. Your mother wants you to find it before the cleaning lady does."

"Me? How? And if it's so important, why doesn't she do it herself?"

"I'm just passing on the message." The man looked anxiously behind us as if the woman he was so afraid of would appear at any moment. "But if you don't want to do this, just go home where you belong. That's my advice. Your mother can change things all by herself without involving you. If she really thinks she has to."

"Are you a friend of Mom's or not? You tell me what she wants, then tell me to ignore it. And I'm supposed to trust you?"

"Don't trust me! I don't care! I did what I said I would and that's it! Sometimes I think your mother is crazy. Sometimes I know she is!" Morton stood up, wiping his sweaty face with a large lavender handkerchief. "Good day, mademoiselle!" He stuffed the kerchief back in his pocket and hurried off.

I wanted to chase after him. He was the only link I had to Mom. But was he a good link or a bad one? I had no idea. What if everything he had said was a complete lie? Did Mom really care about Dreyfus that much? Was his life the change she meant?

I could assume that much was true because of her letter, but did she really expect me to sneak into an embassy office? Was I supposed to knock out the cleaning woman and take her place? That sounded like the kind of thing that would happen in a spy movie. But was it something I could do? And could I get to 1894 to do it?

Or was this whole thing a setup by Morton? Was he an evil

time-traveler like the beautiful creepy woman? I didn't think he'd be so scared of her if they were on the same side, but I wasn't sure who or what to believe.

April 7, 1881

Over tea with Claude, Degas chatted about his favorite jockeys, the dancers he'd draw tomorrow, and one particular one that he was recommending Halévy find a position for in the musical theatre. He was so cheerful that I stopped thinking about the crumbling of the French government and how I was supposed to stop it somehow.

"Monsieur Degas," I said. "I was surprised to see you sketch at the races! I never see you paint outside like Monsieur Monet." It was easier to talk about art than why he should like Jews more. I couldn't quite get myself to do that.

"Ah, well, drawing a quick sketch is one thing. Painting is another. You know how I feel about that! If I were the government, I'd have a special brigade of police to protect the public from artists who paint landscapes outside from nature. They don't have to arrest anyone, but a little bird-shot now and then as a warning would be effective."

"Those are your friends you're talking about!"

"I respect Monet, but he's no friend. Now Manet and Renoir, they are true friends, so I forgive them their follies."

"And Claude? He was drawing outside too. And he's Jewish, so how about him?" Ugh, that was clumsy. I was practically asking Degas if he was ready to round up Jews and shove them all into a locked ghetto.

"Claude is Jewish?" Degas raised an eyebrow. "I did not know that. Should I reconsider his position here?"

"No, of course not!" What a mess I was making! Was I getting Claude fired? I shot him a panicked look. Would he ever forgive me? "I thought you didn't care he was Jewish. After all, the Halévy family is Jewish."

"The Halévys *were* Jewish," Degas corrected me. "They are good Christians now. You can hardly fault them for their ancestry. Well, actually, I suppose one could but I, for one, do not."

"Monsieur Degas is teasing you, Mira," Claude said. "He knows perfectly well that I am a Jew. What matters is whether I can draw, and that is something I am still struggling with. And you are an artist yourself, no matter how much you protest. I've seen you drawing in your sketchbook."

I could feel my cheeks turn bright pink. "I told you, those were just notes," I stammered. "I admit I like to draw, but I'm not an artist." Not on the same level as Claude. And certainly not Degas. I would never show either of them my clumsy scrawls. It would be easier to talk about Judaism than that!

Anyway, Degas was tolerant enough with Jews, and nothing I said made a difference one way or another. If he wanted to support Dreyfus, he would. If he didn't, he wouldn't. I suppose that meant I should think about the second task Mom had given me, at least according to Morton, but that would mean finding a touchstone that would somehow get me to 1894.

Claude walked me home after Degas left for the theater. It all felt so normal that I almost forgot I didn't belong in this time or place. It was easier to think about Claude than time travel and urgent secret missions. Neither of us said anything, but it was a comfortable silence, the kind that holds you like a soft blanket.

"Let's walk through the *jardin*," Claude suggested. "Paris has a lot of fountains, but my favorite is in here." He steered me through the paths lined with rosebushes to an impressive but strange fountain. In front of the spouts of water crouched a sculpture of a lion eating someone's foot.

"I like the lion but why is it devouring a foot?" I asked.

Claude shrugged. "I think that is meant to be naturalistic."

"It seems anything but natural to me!"

"You don't like it?" Claude sounded disappointed.

"Of course I do! I love it! Thank you for showing it to me."

"Perhaps you want to add it to your collection," he suggested.

"What do you mean? My collection of what?"

"Drawings. Go ahead and sketch it. I won't look." Something soft in his face and voice encouraged me. And he was right. My fingers were itching to draw it. I had thought I'd sketch it from my memory, later alone in my room, the way I usually did, but now the temptation was too great. I opened my sketchbook and started to draw.

Claude kept his word and didn't look, but he was so sweet and patient, waiting for me to finish, that I did something I never thought I'd do. I showed him the drawing.

"Mira, this is wonderful! You have such an expressive line, so full of life! And you said you were not an artist." Claude looked up from the page, gazing directly into my eyes.

"It's nothing, really," I murmured, embarrassed.

"No, it is a definite something. You have a real talent, you know. Thank you so much for letting me see this."

Something shifted between us at that moment. We hadn't kissed, hadn't even held hands, but there was an intimacy between us, as soft and warm and welcoming as I'd imagined a kiss could be.

"There is something else I would like to show you," Claude said, his voice hushed and low.

"Yes?" My voice quavered.

"I…" he leaned forward, his gaze intent on mine.

"Yes?" I remembered how his lips felt on my wrist.

He leaned closer still and I tipped my lips up to meet his. He stepped forward and I don't know why, but I stumbled, bumping into the lion. A jolt went through me, my stomach lurched, my eyes glazed over, and the park whirled around me in greens, golds, blues, and browns. Suns rose and set rapidly, and when the ground stopped tilting, I was still in the park but Claude was gone. I must have found my touchstone—at the absolute worst minute. When I definitely wasn't looking for it at all.

Winter?

It was cold, the grass rimed with frost, and my dress far too thin for the biting chill. I didn't see any cars or satellite dishes so it wasn't 2012. I was still in the past. I walked toward Mary Cassatt's apartment, and everything seemed much the same as in 1881.

The same but not the same. The little grocery store Claude and I had just passed was now a butcher shop. But the newsstand was still there, and so were the bakery and the music hall with the lanterns hanging outside.

The hats in the milliner's window were similar, the dresses and shoes in familiar styles, so not enough time had passed

for fashion to change. A play-bill announced the opera *Carmen*, music by Georges Bizet, libretto by Ludovic Halévy. Halevy, Degas's friend! So still the 1880s, I bet. Then I noticed the date on the poster, January 1895! Mom wanted me to go to

1894. I'd skipped past when I was supposed to go. But I hadn't meant to time-travel at all. I had no control on how to make it work. What was I supposed to do now that I was here?

I walked aimlessly in a daze. All I wanted was to be back with my family in the right place at the right time. How could I trust I would ever have a future when time kept changing around me? I felt totally lost.

The streets grew more crowded, and I found myself jostled by children running and yelling, men rushing, even women joining the throng. Everyone was heading in the same direction. I tried to read from people's expressions what was happening.

Some looked furious, others excited. Some had a strange look I couldn't quite place. Almost like happiness but with a nasty edge to it. A whirlpool of people swirled around me, pushing, pulling, shoving. What was going on?

I stopped one woman who looked eager, like she was rushing to some kind of big giveaway at a store opening. I held on to her sleeve, forcing her to answer me when I asked in faltering French where she was going.

"To the Military College, of course! Everyone wants to be there!" Her eyes moist with excitement, she pulled away and ran off before I could ask why anyone would care about a military academy. So I followed the hordes. I really didn't have a choice anyway. Waves of shoulders and arms carried me along. I couldn't have thrust my way across or through them even if I'd wanted to. I tried not to panic, nearly crushed by the bodies around me. A boot stomped on my dress, tearing the hem. An elbow thrust into my ribs.

The crowd got thicker and meaner as we neared a familiar spire. It was the Eiffel Tower! It gleamed shiny and new in the winter light. Maybe that was what everyone was so excited about.

But why the anger? Because the mass of people had turned into a furious mob. They turned their backs to the Eiffel Tower, surging instead toward a big building facing it across a long green. Now they were chanting, pumping angry fists over their heads, mouths twisted in scowls. Some even threw rocks, though what they were trying to hit was invisible to me.

The roar became words and as I understood what they were saying, a horrible dark fear plummeted through me.

"Kill the Jews! Kill the Jews! Kill the Jews!"

This wasn't the right time for the Holocaust, and I thought pogroms were something that happened in Eastern Europe, not France. What horrible moment of the past was I trapped in?

People were pushed up against the gates of the building facing the Eiffel Tower. I frantically made out the inscription along the front—this was the War College the woman had talked about, the goal of the surging mob. Some climbed on top of carriage roofs; others perched in trees, craning to see inside the courtyard. I could hear a military drumroll from the other side of the gate, and I found myself pressed between a large man, his face red with rage, spittle flying from his lips, and a wiry woman, snarling and hooting like a crazy fiend. Squeezed between their sweaty bodies, I was shoved into the barred gate with a view of rows of soldiers, all standing at attention.

A man was led in front of all the ranks, clearly a prisoner even though he wore a uniform. Facing a row of officers, he held his head high, light glinting off his glasses. He looked small and slender, frail in his isolation in front of the massed rows of soldiers. For a second I thought he was the man who'd been with Mom at the racecourse. But I was too far away to really tell.

The officer facing him declared loudly, "Captain Alfred Dreyfus, you have been found guilty of treason and will be punished accordingly. You no longer deserve to wear the rank or uniform of a soldier."

It was Dreyfus! It was too late to save him and now here he was, being publicly stripped of his rank. The people around me jeered and hissed, drowning out the officer's words.

"Down with the traitor! Down with the Jew! Death to Dreyfus!"

I felt sick to my stomach, forced to witness the exact thing Mom had wanted me to prevent. It was all so ugly! I'd never seen the brute force of a mob before, like an out-of-control fire raging wildly. And I hope I never see it again.

But even as people heckled and spat, I could hear Dreyfus, more forceful than their hatred. "I am innocent!" he yelled. "I am innocent! Long live France!"

Even as a soldier stripped the trim off his hat, ripped the epaulets from his shoulders, cut the buttons from his uniform, Dreyfus held his head up, proudly insisting on his innocence. Then the soldier took the sword from the prisoner's side and broke it over his knee with a loud crack.

"Death to Dreyfus! Death to the Jew!" the mob screamed, driven to a greater frenzy by the echoing snap of broken steel.

The red-faced man on my left pushed me into the screaming woman on my other side. She clawed at me furiously, thrusting me into another man's back. I had to get away, to breathe fresh air, to stop the pawing, mauling hands and elbows, shoulders, and boots. But everywhere I turned there was another furious fist, screeching mouth, stomping foot. I was terrified, alone in the crowd of angry bodies.

Then the drums started rat-a-tat-tatting again. The people around me quieted down as if waiting for something dramatic and awful to happen to the prisoner. I covered my eyes, afraid to look, afraid not to. But the officers were finished. Dreyfus was marched away along the columns of soldiers, back into the depths of the War College. His uniform was in ratty shreds now, but he still held his head high.

Slowly the crowd drifted away. I could go where I wanted to now, but I had nowhere to go, nothing to do. I couldn't stop shaking.

Could I get back to 1894 like Mom had wanted, make it so this horrible scene never happened? Or was it too late and I'd missed my chance? The whole thing with Dreyfus had seemed so distant before, but now I knew he was a real person, somebody with the strength to face viciousness with courage. I would have crumpled onto the ground, like I wanted to do now. I never would have been able to be so defiant. Maybe that's why I hadn't been able to save him. I wasn't brave enough.

I sat down, exhausted, on the grass stretching out from the

Eiffel Tower. I was still in the past, so there must be something I could still change. I could still make a difference. I had to!

Maybe I could go back to Mom's first idea and get Degas to support Dreyfus so that there would be a public outcry for a new trial. I wasn't sure what else to do. But I had to try something, so I headed back the way I'd come hours before.

By the time I got to Montmartre, I felt numb and hollow. All I could think of was getting warm. I hurried to Mary Cassatt's apartment, hoping it was still hers, hoping she was home. She wasn't, but the servant let me in. The same servant from before, though older, of course. I wondered if I was older too.

"Mademoiselle! You'll catch your death! Let me draw you a hot bath and you can warm yourself up while you're waiting for the mistress."

I sank into the water, washing away the mob's ugly hatred. I was so drained that I could barely keep my eyes open, but whenever I closed them, I saw the sneering faces, heard the hoarse screams, only this time the Jew the crowd wanted to kill was me.

January 6, 1895

I must have fallen alseep after the bath because I woke up to find myself in the familiar guest bed at Mary Cassatt's. Yesterday was a foggy nightmare. Today would be fresh and new, if a day so long ago in the past could be called new.

I looked in the mirror, afraid I'd have gray hairs and wrinkles, but I was still me, exactly the same. This was 1895, fourteen years since I was last in Paris. Would anyone think it strange I hadn't aged? What about Claude? He was probably married with children by now. He would have forgotten me completely. But I would never forget him. Or the kiss I almost got.

I wanted to go see Degas and Claude right away, but I waited until Mary woke up so I could talk to her. There had to be a reason I was here now, why I'd skipped 1894 entirely. Maybe because Morton had been lying. My job had to be meant for this time, so I needed to figure out what that was. All I knew was that it had to do with Degas, the Jews, and Dreyfus. And Zola, whoever that was, since Mom's note said she would "work on him." How could I ask Mary about that?

"Mira? How extraordinary to see you again after so many years! And you haven't changed a bit. Americans always look younger and fresher than Europeans, but you're exceptional, unbelievable, truly." Mary poured me a cup of coffee as we sat down for breakfast.

"You haven't aged at all either," I gushed, though really she had. Her features were softer, droopier, her waist thicker and her hands knottier, but there was also a self-assurance about her that made her more attractive than ever. And looking at the canvases leaning against the walls, the prints framed everywhere, I could see why. Her art was stronger—her pastels as rich as Degas, her lines as sure.

"How are your parents? Your sister? The last time we talked, she was ill."

I tried to remember her sister's name. Leona? Louisa? Something that started with "L."

"So kind of you to remember. Poor Lydia died." Mary dabbed at her eyes with a handkerchief.

"Oh, I'm so sorry!" I gasped.

"I still miss her, though it's been twelve years now." Mary sighed.

I stared at my lap miserably, searching for the right thing to say. I couldn't imagine Malcolm dying. Suddenly I missed my brother with a sharp intensity.

"Let's talk about something more cheerful, shall we?" Mary proposed. "Like art. Or better yet, artists."

"You must tell me how our friend Degas is doing!" I grabbed the chance to change the subject. "And what the news of the day is." I paused, hoping I sounded natural, not idiotic. "I've been wondering about Zola…and Dreyfus."

"Degas is much the same, ever the crochety perfectionist. Manet's death hit him hard, but he's doing well. You can see for yourself. We can meet him for tea tomorrow."

More death! I thought, but I wasn't going to ask for details about Manet's. Instead I asked, "Does Claude still work for him?"

"Claude? Why, of course! He's devoted to Degas."

I wanted to ask if he was married. If he was a successful painter himself now. If he remembered me at all. But I wasn't here for Claude. I was here for Mom.

"And what about Zola?" I asked, getting right to the point. "And this Dreyfus I've heard so much about?" I wondered what she knew. I couldn't imagine she'd been part of yesterday's savage crowd. Being here with her was like being in another Paris entirely.

"The last thing I read of Zola's was the dreadful novel he wrote skewering poor Cézanne, you know, *The Masterpiece*. Degas was disgusted that Zola could betray their friendship that way, though secretly I think he agrees with Zola that Cézanne could be a better artist and he hasn't lived up to his promise."

At least now I knew who Zola was, though I couldn't see what he had to do with anything, why Mom had to work on him. He was a writer of bad books. Why did that matter?

"And Dreyfus?" I pressed.

"Hmm, you know, that name rings a bell, though he's not someone I know. Not an artist, that's certain. I know! I read something recently...It was in the newspaper, today's, I think." Mary flipped through a pile of magazines and journals on a nearby table.

"Here it is!" She folded back the page and handed me the newspaper.

Next to the article was an illustration of Dreyfus. The artist had sketched him with an exaggerated nose and devil's horns, nothing like the man I'd seen act so nobly the day before. Would the article help me understand why the mob was so furious? And, more importantly, would it tell me what I needed to do next?

My stomach clenched as I read about Dreyfus being found guilty of treason. Then the writer described the ceremony I'd seen. Except according to the newspaper, Dreyfus was barely human, more demon than man. If I was supposed to make Degas like Jews, then I guessed my job was to make Degas help prove he was innocent. But seeing anti-Semitism in person, it didn't seem like changing people's minds would be easy.

These were real people, real lives being ruined. How could people read about such injustice and not be outraged? Even if they believed that Dreyfus was guilty, how could they present him as a demon? To the newspaper writer, he seemed barely human.

If I couldn't clear Dreyfus's name somehow, that would be my job—to show the public that Dreyfus was accused simply because he was Jewish. And that he was a man like any other, not some kind of evil monster. I had no idea how I would do that, but I was so angry I had to figure something out. I didn't care about changing something in the future. What mattered was this right now, this ugly anti-Semitism.

"Of course, you're welcome to stay here as long as you like. It will be nice to have the company."

I looked up from the newspaper, from the horrible caricature of the demon Jew to Mary's kind face. She'd never said anything about me being Jewish, and suddenly that really mattered to me.

"That's so generous of you!" I said, folding over the paper so I couldn't see the ugly drawing. "You must have thought me rude, leaving like that without saying good-bye or thanking you after all your kind hospitality."

"Actually I thought you must have run off with a young man. Claude thought so too."

I blushed hotly. "Nothing like that! My aunt called for me urgently, and I had to hurry to catch a train. I did write to you from Italy, but it sounds like you didn't get my letter. The post can be so unreliable," I lied.

"Yes, terrible really, since your letter to Monsieur Degas was also lost." Mary's eyes twinkled. She clearly didn't believe a word I'd said, but she didn't seem to care that I was an ungrateful liar.

I'd dug myself a hole and felt myself falling deeper. What a nuisance this time-travel stuff was! How did Mom handle all the lame excuses and clumsy lies? If I didn't care about these people, it wouldn't matter, but I wanted Mary, Degas, and Claude to like me. Or at least not think I was a horrible person.

I could almost hear Mom's voice in my head saying, "Stop worrying about your reputation. It doesn't matter what other people think of you—it matters what you think of you." Right now I thought of myself as someone who wanted very much to be friends with Mary. And Degas. I wasn't sure about Claude. After all, I'd disappeared just as he was going to kiss me (wasn't he?). That would be pretty hard to explain away.

Degas had moved to a bigger place, not far from his old apartment, and when I got there he was sketching a woman

crouched in a tub washing herself. His marks were looser and thicker than I remembered. I could lose myself in their energy and beating pulse, as his fingers skated over the paper. He leaned into the drawing, peering closely at it as if he needed glasses, even though he was already wearing a pair perched on his nose.

"Mira?" he asked, turning toward me. "It has been years! I thought you had decided to stay in America and abandon your French friends."

"I'm so sorry that I left the way I did. You must think I'm awful." I watched the colors bloom under his fingers as if I was in a trance. I'd never seen him draw like this before. It felt intensely private and magical.

"I would say it is good to see you, but as you can tell, I do not see well at all these days. My eyesight has long been poor, and now it is so impoverished that it needs to beg for pennies on the street." He threw down the chalks. "Enough for today, Mireille. You can dress and go."

"Please don't stop. I love to watch you draw." The spell was broken, but the sketch was still there, raw and unfinished but powerful all the same.

"Watch me draw?" Degas barked a short laugh. "Art isn't a spectator sport. It's the finished piece that matters."

I didn't agree with him and thought the privilege of seeing

him create was just as important as the finished drawing itself. Still, I didn't want to be a nuisance. I couldn't sketch if someone was looking over my shoulder. "I didn't want to interrupt you," I said, sitting down next to Degas, my eyes still on his picture. "I was just eager to see you after so many years."

"Me? What about poor Claude? He took your leaving rather hard, you know."

He did? He cared about me? My face flushed pink with embarrassment. And then I felt awful—I'd hurt Claude! He must have thought I had run away from his kiss. I was terrible at this time-travel stuff. Why had Mom called this a gift? It didn't feel like one. I struggled to find something believable to say to Degas to explain my horrible behavior.

"You must believe me that it was urgent, I didn't want to, but I had to go. I had no time to say good-bye." I could barely meet Degas's eyes. He must despise me. "I wish I could take it all back and do things differently, really I do." For once I was telling the truth.

"You do not owe me an apology. Your life is yours to do with as you please."

"But it wasn't as I pleased! I wanted to stay here with you, with Claude!" I tried not to cry, but just then Claude walked in with Degas's lunch and I couldn't stop the tears from gushing.

He was a man now, taller, filled out, with a beard, but it was definitely him. He saw me and froze.

"Mira?" He looked astonished and anguished at once.

I swallowed my tears and wiped my eyes. "Oh, Claude, please forgive me! I didn't want to leave, but I did, and you haven't heard from me in so long!"

"Mira, it really is you!" Claude put down the sandwiches wrapped in newspaper he'd brought for lunch. He knelt next to me and handed me his handkerchief. "Do not cry! We are not angry with you, are we, Degas?"

"I was never angry with Mira, not for a second," Degas said. "I thought you had gone to America to bring me back a turkey buzzard. Have you?"

I sniffled but couldn't help smiling. "Again with the turkey buzzards," I murmured. I was wearing the same dress as when we were together in the park, that day of the almost-kiss. I wondered if Claude remembered.

"It is astonishing! You are precisely the same. Precisely!"

"Oh, these Americans," Degas drawled. "They are a young country, you know. Babies, all of them. It is the same in Tahiti. Gauguin writes that the women there simply do not age the way our French country lasses do. As if the more primitive way they live smooths away wrinkles, vanquishes gray hair. But in any case youth is overrated. Anyone can be a genius at twenty-five. The trick is to be one at fifty."

He was talking as if nothing had changed, as if I hadn't vanished for more than a decade and turned up out of nowhere. I wanted to throw my arms around his neck and kiss him in gratitude.

"So you forgive me?"

"There is nothing to forgive, is there, Claude?" Degas gave him one of his rare smiles.

"Of course not! We hope this time you can stay."

"I hope so too," I said. I really did. For a minute I forgot what time I belonged in. It was tempting to think I could stay here with Claude for good. But he was already too old for me. And I wasn't a nineteenth-century Parisian. I had to remind myself I was here for a reason. Mom was counting on me.

"You only hope? You do not know?" Claude looked anxious again.

"It's my aunt. She called me away suddenly and I had to go, and I meant to write but things got complicated, and I don't know what will happen next." I offered the same lame excuse I'd given Mary.

"Leave her be, Claude. She is a free woman, and can come and go as she pleases."

"Then how long are you here for?" Claude pressed.

"I don't know. I'm not sure yet. It depends." I'd run out of explanations and desperately needed to change the subject. "Let's talk about something else, shall we? What do you think of the Dreyfus case?"

"A wretched man to betray his country like that, hardly an earthshaking story," Degas said, not at all fazed by my question.

He tossed me a newspaper, a different one than Mary's. "You can read about the horrid man here. If you excuse me, I must wash the chalks from my hands and change into more presentable clothes."

Now that I was alone with Claude, the room didn't seem sunny and warm, but tense and edgy. He sat in the chair next to me, arranging Degas's simple lunch while keeping his eyes glued to me as if he was afraid I'd disappear right in front of him. I scanned the newspaper with one eye while I tried to look like I was paying complete attention to him. It was a technique I'd perfected in school when a teacher was particularly boring and I didn't want her to know I was engrossed in a book on my lap instead of listening to her drone.

This article was just as ugly in how it described the evil Dreyfus, but this time the writer wrote about the coming punishment, how the traitor would be shackled to a cot in solitary confinement in a small prison built especially for him on Devil's Island, an old leper colony off the coast of South America that the French used for convicts. I couldn't imagine anything that Degas could possibly say, even if he wanted to, that would convince the public that Dreyfus was innocent. How could Mom have thought that would work? What was I really supposed to do here? How could I make people outraged at an injustice when they saw Dreyfus as the demon Jew who deserved the most severe punishment possible?

"I thought you were angry at me," Claude interrupted my thoughts. "The way you left without a word. I thought maybe  I had pushed you to show me something you did not want to reveal. So now you have forgiven me?"

"I was never angry at you!" I didn't for a minute regret letting Claude see my sketchbook. He had encouraged me, and in return, I'd hurt him. I wished I could tell him the truth. Instead I lied, as usual.

"It was my aunt, like I said." What a lame excuse! I wouldn't blame him if he hated me.

I tried to meet Claude's eyes, to let him know how truly sorry I was, but his face was turned away, his jaw tight. There was a distance between us, not just because so many years had passed for him but because obviously I was still so young and he was a grown-up. No more chance of kisses. I wondered if we could even still be friends.

January 8, 1895

Mary invited me to join her and a group of artists at the Nouvelles Athènes, a nearby café. Degas was there, as was Claude. He nodded when he saw me, but the old warmth was gone. I'd ruined that friendship. Not that I'd meant to. Maybe if I was better at time travel, I could have done things differently.

Morton never did explain how I could control this "gift." And Mom hadn't either. I wondered if I'd ever get it right. Was time travel like drawing, something you had to do over and over to do well? That was a scary thought! I've been drawing since I could hold a crayon, and I'm still nowhere near as good as I want to be.

Then I had an even scarier thought—maybe Mom was more experienced at time travel than I was, but she still wasn't good enough to control it either. Maybe she didn't know how to get home. Maybe we were both stuck in the past.

I tried not to think about that as Degas introduced me to a middle-aged man with a neatly trimmed moustache and beard who was dressed in white flannel with a beret perched jauntily on his head.

"Mira, this is Émile Zola." So here was the notorious writer at last! He seemed so ordinary, except for the unusual

choice in clothes (white flannel?), yet somehow he was really important to Mom. Important to both of us then. Because somehow if we did something right with him, we'd both go back home. I just had to figure out what that thing was and trust that Mom was a better time-traveler than I was an artist.

"Another American niece of yours, I presume," Zola said in thickly accented English.

"No, no, Mira is a friend. My brother, René, the one in New Orleans, sent his daughter to stay with me for several months a couple of years ago. You can see how much she improved my English. A lovely girl! It is so important to have family, you know. I regret that I never married, but the thought of a wife criticizing my painting was more than I could bear. Remember how much Madame Manet harped on poor Manet?"

"Remember how he cut up your portrait of the two of them because you didn't do justice to her…ahem…beauty?"

"Given her actual face, I did the best I could!"

"Well, you could have had a wife like Madame Renoir, a sweet cream puff of a woman," observed Zola.

"But I would have had to be a sweet cream puff of a man, like our friend Renoir. No, a bitter, old curmudgeon like me would have ended up with a shrill harpy. I cannot change who I am."

"Nor would we want you to, though we all fear your sharp wit," said a man with bright button eyes and a moustache so big it covered half his face. I wondered if he was hiding something in all that hair—a dueling scar or a massive pimple.

"I thought Oscar Wilde could be cutting. Then I met you!" he continued. The man was James Whistler, an American painter who had moved to Paris. Degas introduced me to

him, praising his etchings, but to me he was the guy who painted that famous picture of his mother in a rocking chair, the one that's a recurring joke in cartoons.

"I don't know Renoir well, but he didn't strike me as such a cream puff," I said.

"Compared to Degas he is!" Mary laughed. "Renoir knows how to relax. Degas knows only how to make art."

"That is not true!" Degas objected. "I go to the theater, the opera, the ballet all the time. Almost every night!"

"And then you go straight home to bed," teased Whistler. "Paris is known for its clubs and dance halls but you don't take advantage of them."

"I leave that to Toulouse-Lautrec," said Degas. "He can have them!"

"You admire his paintings then?" Zola asked.

"Actually, I do. His posters for the Moulin Rouge have the look of Japanese prints."

"I agree with you, Degas." Zola nodded. "In fact, I was thinking that he would make the perfect illustrator for a new book I'm thinking about."

"A book?" I squeaked. Wasn't he supposed to write about Dreyfus? Wasn't that what Mom wanted? If she wanted Degas to support Dreyfus, that had to be what she wanted Zola to do.

"Monsieur Zola is a writer, not an artist," Degas explained. "Perhaps he is not yet translated into English. Are you, Zola?"

"I should hope so!" he huffed. "How else would Whistler know my work?"

"That is why painting is superior to writing—no translation necessary," Whistler said.

Mary was describing a literary magazine she and Degas were working on when a woman walking down the street caught my eye. Something about the way she moved was deeply familiar. As she came closer, I could make out her deep blue dress, her hat, her hair. It was Mom!

I slid down in my chair, turning so she wouldn't see me. I held my breath, waiting for her to come closer, ready to run after her if she walked by. Maybe I could at least slip her a note? I wanted desperately to hug her, to hold tight and never let her go, but all I could do was sneak glances at her.

"Émile! There you are!" she called out to Zola. Her familiar voice stabbed me. I couldn't help it. I burst into tears.

"Mira, what's wrong?" Claude took my hand. I kept my head turned away, but Mom must have heard my name. She froze where she stood, so close I could almost reach out and grab her.

"I'm so sorry, Émile! We'll talk later. We have much to discuss." Mom's voice cracked with fear. She was terrified. Of me? I hated to think that. It had to be the stupid rule. Whatever it was, she turned and dashed away, disappearing between the ragpickers, vegetable peddlers, and washerwomen with baskets of clothes.

I felt sick to my stomach. I wanted to help Mom, but I'd

made things worse. I'd gotten in the way of her convincing Zola of anything, which meant now I'd have to do it instead. I had to figure out how he could support Dreyfus. What could he do that would make a difference? I tried to focus on the problem, but first I needed to calm down. I wiped away the tears and drank the water Claude offered me.

"Mira, your hands are shaking. You aren't well. Should I walk you home?"

He was so sweet to me that I wanted to lean into his chest and let him comfort me. But he couldn't really be my friend. And I had to help Mom.

"I'm fine," I told him. "I just swallowed something wrong, got some dust in my eye." I was the master of the lame excuse. Next I'd tell him the dog had eaten my homework.

"So strange for Serena to act that way," Zola was saying. "She was supposed to bring me some useful information, but it's just as well. I don't want to think about writing anything for a while."

So that's what Zola needed to do—write something about Dreyfus. Surely not a book. Those took too long to be printed to make much of a difference. Unless publishing was a lot quicker in the nineteenth century than in the twenty-first. I was trying to think of a clever way to bring up the Dreyfus case when Whistler did it for me.

"You know, the English press thinks a charge as serious as

treason should be tried openly. None of this secret evidence you French are so fond of. What's fascinating to me is the way your newspapers report the whole thing, as if there's no question but the man must be guilty."

"Because there is no doubt of it!" Degas snapped, his face suddenly rigid. He'd transformed into a cold aristocrat in a second. Maybe this was why he had a reputation as such a grump.

"There's precious little proof, seems to me," Whistler insisted. "There's the handwriting that some experts say is Dreyfus's while others say it isn't. There's no motive, since the man had independent financial means."

"Being Jewish with ties to Alsace-Lorraine is motive enough!"

"Then accuse all the Jews in the military!" Whistler laughed. "It's ridiculous!"

"How many Jews do you think there are in the service?" scoffed Degas. "Theirs is a vile race of cowards."

I'd never seen this side of Degas. It was like learning that somebody you liked and admired advocated slavery or thought women shouldn't be allowed to vote. Could I like someone who said such hateful things? I looked at Claude, wondering if he felt the same way. His jaw was tense, his eyes angry, his hands tight fists. I couldn't help myself. I leaned forward and whispered in his ear.

"We don't have to listen to this. We can go."

He pulled away. He wasn't going to leave, and I was proud of him for that. "Dreyfus," he declared, "is a scapegoat." Everyone was staring at Claude now. Degas looked furious. But Claude didn't back down. "And when the real traitor is found, he will be vindicated. It is only a matter of time." His voice was strong and firm. And just being next to him, I felt filled with a new sense of purpose. Mom was right—we had to help Dreyfus.

Degas could forgive my sudden departure, my return out of nowhere, but I wasn't sure he'd forgive Claude this. Had he just lost his place in the artist's household? I was worried for him. But if he was willing to talk, so was I.

"Monsieur Whistler," I said, "you've clearly read a lot about this case, and I'm curious if you can explain it better to me. I really don't know what it's about."

"The worst is the secret file, the evidence that Dreyfus wasn't allowed to refute because he was not allowed to see it. You as an American can appreciate the basic tenet of law that an accused has the right to answer his accuser and examine the evidence used to convict him. Some sources even say that the file is completely invented, not a word of truth in it, just suppositions and circumstantial evidence of the thinnest kind."

"If he's not allowed to see it, that makes it even easier to invent, doesn't it?" I asked.

"The military does not make up evidence!" Degas snapped. "The very idea is ridiculous!"

"But if it was invented?" I pressed.

"It was not!" Degas looked furious now. I was afraid to say anything else, but Whistler wasn't.

"I think it's precisely the kind of thing the military would do. Without clear evidence, they would feel compelled to create some. They wanted an open-and-shut case, so they made one."

"Who could have written such a file? Who was in charge?" I turned toward Whistler, my back to Degas.

"I suppose anyone could have made up lies, but I've heard that a counterintelligence agent named Hubert-Joseph Henry is behind some kind of file on Dreyfus, maybe this secret one." Whistler leaned back with a broad grin. "You have to go to England to get all the facts. They won't print them here in France!"

"Pfffttt!" Degas snorted. "As if British journalism is so pure!"

"In this case it is!" huffed Whistler.

"Back to this Henry fellow," I interrupted. "If I wanted to talk to him, where would I find him?"

Whistler peered at me from under his bushy eyebrows. "You want to talk to him? Are you a girl reporter from the *New York Herald* in disguise? Try the War Ministry or the War College. And good luck!"

Claude stared at me. "What are you talking about?" he hissed. "Do you know something?"

"Just as much as you know," I whispered back. "I'm trying to learn more."

"What do you think, Zola?" asked Whistler. "You're strangely silent."

"I don't know enough yet to judge. And I'm not sure I should care."

Whistler raised an eyebrow so high it almost floated off his forehead. "Justice is something we should all care about. This affair smells to high heaven and we're not through with it yet, I assure you. This poor Dreyfus fellow has been sent off to Devil's Island, but he'll appeal. If he's innocent, the truth will out and the War Ministry won't look foolish. It will look evil."

As if called up by the word "evil," the woman from the race-track walked into the café. Or should I say "slithered"? She swung her hips in an exaggerated roll, her head proudly high. If I didn't know her, I'd be in awe of her model good looks. But I did know her and my mouth went dry with panic, though I knew she couldn't do anything to me here in public. I glared at her, daring her to make a move.

She shifted her beady eyes from face to face, passing over mine to light on Zola's.

"Monsieur!" she exclaimed, rudely interrupting the conversation. "We've met, but you probably don't remember me. I'm Madame Lefoutre from the Free Press Agency, and we'd love for you to write something about the despicable traitor who has stained with his vileness the uniform he wore. Treason is, after all, a serious offense, one the public should be quick to condemn."

"Madame, I assure you, if I'd met you before, I would remember," Zola said. "A man doesn't forget such beauty!"

"Are you referring to Dreyfus or to the military court that condemned him on so little evidence?" Whistler asked, clearly not as charmed by Madame Lefoutre's looks as Zola was.

"To Dreyfus, of course!" she snapped.

"And your little dog too!" I couldn't resist saying. She sounded so much like Miss Gulch, about to scoop up Toto and stuff the dog into the basket on her bicycle.

"Dog? What are you talking about? Dreyfus, yes, he's a dog, an ugly mongrel of the lowest breeding," Madame Lefoutre-my-foot said.

"Alas, I'm not the kind of writer you're looking for." Zola sighed, ignoring Whistler's jibes and my random remarks. "I write novels, not journalism."

"She thinks you owe the army an apology since you wrote that rabble-rousing book criticizing their corruption and in-eptitude in the military years ago," Whistler said.

"Rabble-rousing?" I asked. That's what Zola needed to do for Dreyfus!

"My radical days are over." Zola sipped his wine. "That is what youth is for. Now I'm a respectable citizen."

"Then you should want to write a defense of the army!" Madame Lefoutre insisted. I'll give her this, she didn't give up easily.

"I write what I choose, not what others tell me to write." Zola smiled. "Even when the request comes from such luscious lips that it is hard to refuse."

"Did I mention that we'll pay—quite generously, I should add?"

"Not nearly enough, Madame." Zola stood up. "I'm sorry, but I must be going now."

Madame Lefoutre followed him out but he gave her a double-cheek kiss, hailed a cab, and climbed inside. I wondered if I could be any more convincing about writing something *for* Dreyfus rather than against. I didn't have any of Madame's formidable powers of flirtation or money. What could I possibly offer him?

"I'm sorry she left," Whistler said dryly. "I was about to ask her to model for me. She's the very picture of Greed and Cruelty in their oh-so-deceptive beauty."

Degas frowned. "Who wants to paint such blandness? I prefer faces with that saving touch of ugliness, that detail that gives character, that makes a face truly interesting." When he said that, I wanted to hug him. It was the kind of thing that made me like him so much, even though he was so wrong about Dreyfus. He might agree with Madame politically, but that didn't mean he liked her.

"That, my friend, we can all agree on. Let's drink to Character, to the Truly Interesting!" Whistler held up his glass. Mary, Claude, and Degas all lifted theirs.

So maybe Claude wouldn't be fired as Degas's assistant if they could all drink together after such a heated argument. I didn't stay to find out, though. I had to find Hubert-Joseph Henry. And thanks to Whistler, I had an idea of where. I wasn't eager to go back to the War College, but this time there'd be no mob. Just me and a chance to set things right.

January 9, 1895

I circled the War Ministry and the War College, tried to get into both places, but each time I was turned away. I waited outside the War College for hours, staring across the green at the Eiffel Tower. Funny to think it hadn't been here when I was last in Paris in 1881, and now here it was, that landmark everyone associated with the city.

I waited so long that I had time to invent a whole story to explain myself, using Degas's family as an example. I planned on introducing myself as a long-lost cousin from the American branch of Henry's family and saying I was tracking him down because he had come into an inheritance. If he thought he would get something valuable from me, he'd want to talk. If I got that far.

"Go home, girlie," barked the guard. "No visitors allowed."

"I'm not visiting. I'm waiting."

A carriage rolled up and the guard snapped to attention. A thick man in an elaborate uniform with gold braid epaulets and buttons, shiny high boots, and a Napoleonic hat stepped out.

"Excuse me, sir," I said, rushing up before the guard could shoo me away. "I'm looking for Hubert-Joseph Henry, an officer here. It's urgent that I speak with him. This guard has refused to let me pass."

"And you are?" the man asked gruffly. His face wasn't kind at all, but severe and shut off, as if he saw only the things he wanted to see—and I wasn't one of them.

I launched into my story. "I'm a relative of his from New Orleans. My mother told me to find him here. I have some important news to deliver to him."

"Is the news military?" snapped the man. "I think not! Then you can find Monsieur Henry at home."

"Now go!" roared the guard.

I went, but not so far that I couldn't see Henry when he left, if he was there in the first place. I didn't know what he looked like, but I figured I'd approach every officer until I found the right one. Except long minutes stretched by and nobody came out. Or went in. I'd almost dozed off when I heard another carriage roll up to the entry. It waited there until a man came out of the War College. His uniform was less elaborate than the gruff man's, but he still looked like an officer.

"Lieutenant Colonel Henry." The guard saluted. "A young lady was here looking for you. Said she's from your family in America."

"America?" Henry frowned. "I have no relatives in America." He stepped into the carriage.

Two more men followed him, but the strange thing was that although they carried themselves rigidly like soldiers, neither of them wore military uniforms. One was tall with a big bushy beard, and as I peered at him, I realized that it hooked over  his ears, like a disguise. The other was short with blue-tinted glasses, like props in some play.

"Come on, Henry, let's go!" the short one yelled, leaning out of the carriage to thump on the door. "*Allez-y!*"

Could I keep up with a carriage? I had to try. I must have looked strange holding up my skirts and jogging along behind them, but they couldn't see me and I didn't care about anybody else. When the horse trotted, I had to run to keep pace, but when it got crowded and the horse slowed to a walk, I had a chance to catch my breath. Luckily for me, it was late in the day, the streets were thronged, and the horse was forced to walk most of the time.

The carriage slowed to a stop in front of the Jardin du Luxembourg. Fake Beard and Blue Glasses got out, but they didn't walk away. Instead they leaned against the carriage and waited. For who or what I had no idea.

I thought of approaching Hubert-Joseph Henry then, but decided to see what they were waiting for first. I stood by the park gate, pretending I really was waiting for somebody. If I'd had a watch to check, I would have, but all I could do to mime my impatience was to stomp a foot now and then and mutter, "Where could he be?" I felt like Winnie the Pooh trying to convince the bees that he was an innocent rain cloud so he could grab their honey.

The two men weren't looking at me at all, so I was probably wasting my act, but I kept it up until a third man arrived. Then I inched closer so I could hear what they said.

"Why do you need to see me?" the third man shrilled. He was shorter than Blue Glasses, with ears that stuck out like jug handles and an even bigger mustache than Whistler's.

"Henry's waiting for you in the cab," Fake Beard hissed.

"You idiot!" Blue Glasses snarled. "They found your other note, the shredded one from the German attaché! Dreyfus is on Devil's Island, chained to his bed, guarded day and night, yet you've proven that the traitor is a free man, still passing information to the Germans! Picquart wants you arrested, but fortunately for you, if you hang, so do we all! This isn't about saving your skin but preserving the reputation of the army."

"Then hadn't you better treat me more kindly?" huffed Jug Ears. Or I should say, the real traitor, because obviously that's who he was. This man was the officer selling military secrets to the Germans. And being protected by the French military for his crimes!

I wanted to squeeze into the carriage with Jug Ears. But all I could do was wait like the two men wearing their oh-so-fake disguises. At least now I knew why—they had to be military officers too. But instead of arresting the traitor, they were plotting with him.

The minutes stretched on. People walked by, carriages passed. A girl chased a hoop through the gates and into the park. A small dog yapped, straining eagerly at its leash.

Jug Ears clambered out, smoothing his waistcoat. He tipped his hat at Fake Beard and winked. "You'll be taking care of me now, it seems. So long as I have no worries, you have no worries. Otherwise, we'll all end up covered with mud—you more than me, I should think. Good day, gentlemen!"

Fake Beard clenched his fingers into tight fists. "We have to protect that scum!"

"Calm down," said Blue Glasses. "We're protecting ourselves. Esterházy is innocent and Dreyfus is guilty, and that's that."

Esterházy must be Jug Ears' name. I wanted to write it down to be sure I remembered it, but I didn't have time. The two men were getting into the carriage with Henry. Before it could drive away, I ran up and opened the door.

"Excuse me!" I said. "Monsieur Henry, I need to talk to you!"

The man in uniform leaned forward in his seat. "Who are you? What do you want?"

"Can I talk to you in private, sir? Please, it's urgent! It's a private family matter!"

"This is nonsense!" Fake Beard said.

"Please!" I begged.

Henry looked torn, like he wanted to listen to me, but Fake Beard slammed the door shut, and the carriage lumbered away. At first I could keep up, but as we came to a broad boulevard, the horse broke into a trot.

I stopped at a fountain, trying to catch my breath. It was no use; they were too fast. I sank down by the water, ready to cry in frustration. I could try the War College again tomorrow, or maybe I could write to Henry there and convince him somehow to show the public what was in the secret file. After all, if the evidence was true, it would stand up to scrutiny. If it wasn't, it deserved to be discovered for the fraud it was.

I stared into the water, searching for an idea. The fountain was mock Egyptian, with a palm tree capital in the middle surrounded by four sphinxes. "Can you answer the riddle for me?" I asked the sphinx nearest me. "Can you tell me how to solve this mystery?"

Of course, the sphinx said nothing, but when I stretched out a hand and touched its paw, a shiver run through me. Light and dark blinked past, and I swirled away in the haze of time flooding around me. The fountain was a touchstone.

July 1

I was back at Notre Dame on the walkway with the gargoyles, and Malcolm was standing next to me, grumbling that he was hungry and could we go get some crepes.

I hugged my brother so hard that he squeaked.

"Hey, let go! What's the matter?" He pulled away.

"I'm sorry. I just missed you so much." It was true. I had missed him, though I hadn't let myself think about him or Dad much.

"Dad!" I hugged him tightly, and though he looked as surprised as Malcolm, he hugged me back.

"Are you okay?" Dad asked, looking at me as if I was made of glass and might shatter any second.

"This is going to sound crazy, but I saw Mom. I know where she is." Now they both stared at me as if I had sprouted an extra eye. "It's complicated, but let me explain. Just listen first and then you can think I'm a nut job."

We wound our way back down the circular stone staircase, coming out onto the modern street of the modern city with cars and bicycles and huge tour groups led by banner-waving guides. The city sounded different, with the noise of cars, sirens, cell phones, airplanes overhead, and conversations swirling by in several languages. It even smelled different, less like coal burning, trash, and that distinctive sewage aroma, and more like car exhaust, cigarettes, and something else, something indefinably modern. I wondered if I was sniffing technology, the Internet, all the cell phones buzzing around me.

Dad steered us to a café. It was strange to think I'd been in this city so much longer than they had, but this was still my first meal in modern Paris. There was no easy way to explain the

whole time-travel and Mom thing, so I just started at the beginning and went all the way up to the weird meeting with all the disguised military guys and Esterházy. (Yes! I remembered the traitor's name!)

Dad didn't say anything. He just waited for me to finish my bizarre explanation. Malcolm didn't ask anything until the end when he said, "Really? We're supposed to believe this? C'mon, Mira, what's the joke here?"

"It's not a joke! Dad, you believe me, right? Didn't Mom tell you she could time-travel?" I hoped she had, or no way Dad would believe me either.

To my relief, Dad looked me straight in the eyes and nodded.

"What?" Malcolm gaped, his eyes bugging out. He clearly didn't believe either of us. "You're kidding! You've got to be!"

"It's true," Dad said. "But I thought that was over. She hadn't traveled for such a long time…since we met again in college."

"What do you mean 'again'?" I asked.

"It's complicated, as you know, Mira, but I actually met your mom many times as she was time-traveling, never for very long. I couldn't understand why she'd disappear for so long, so suddenly, without a word of warning. She explained it all when we were both twenty. She told me she was finally in the time where she belonged, where she could stay. And be with me."

"So you must have suspected that's what happened when she went missing. That's why we're here, isn't it, to find Mom?" Now Dad's blind faith in Mom made sense. He knew she hadn't left on purpose, but she hadn't been kidnapped either.

"I admit I hoped she'd find us. The postcard was a clue,

both of time and place—you saw how old the stamp was." Dad rubbed his forehead. He looked worried, not relieved, the way I thought he'd be. "She promised she was through with time travel, that it was too dangerous, so I didn't suspect that at first."

"What do you mean dangerous?" I asked.

"There are rules that have to be followed, and if you don't, there are serious consequences for the future."

I leafed through my sketchbook, hoping Mom's letters were still tucked inside. They were! I unfolded the one Morton had given to me and handed it to Dad.

"She sent me a couple of letters. This first one tells the rules. You're not supposed to take things back, but I think I still have these because they don't belong to the past—they belong to Mom from the future. I've kept my sketchbook the same way. You also can't take people back with you or tell anyone you're from the future. And it's better for family members not to travel in the same time and place. Are those all of them?" I couldn't help thinking there were things Mom hadn't told me, things Morton knew but didn't tell me either for some reason.

Dad gripped the letter, reading it with a frown. "These are some of the rules, but she's leaving out the most important one: you can't change anything in the past. Mom said she traveled like a tourist to see, appreciate, experience, but never to change. She insisted all time travelers had to obey that. That's why she stopped traveling once Malcolm was born. She didn't want to risk doing anything to upset our children's future."

"But that's not what she told me!" I blurted out. "Just the opposite! We're supposed to change what happens to Dreyfus, keep him from being punished as a traitor. She was absolutely clear about that. Look, she says so in her last letter." I gave Dad the other two letters, remembering how sweaty and panicky Morton had been when he gave me Mom's message that day on the bench. He was breaking the most important rule of all— not to change the past—and he knew it. He'd said something about owing Mom a big favor so he felt obligated to repay her, but he sure wasn't comfortable about it.

"Wait," said Malcolm. "This is all going too fast. Why didn't you tell us all this when Mom first disappeared, Dad? Why did you let us worry like that?"

"You would have thought I was crazy."

"Instead you think I'm crazy!" I said.

"No, I know you're not," Dad insisted. "And I bet Malcolm believes you too."

Malcolm shook his head. "I guess I have to. Otherwise, I'm surrounded by crazy people."

"What I need to know is why Mom is trying to change history," Dad said. "There has to be a reason." His face suddenly turned pale, and his eyes widened in fear. "There's only one possible explanation. She knows something horrible is going to happen to one or both of you, and she's trying to stop it. She would disobey such an important rule for only one reason—you guys."

"But she told me this has been her job, changing events so bad things won't happen. And there are other time travelers who try to stop her and her friends." I described Madame Lefoutre, how she attacked me in Notre Dame, how she followed Mom.

"She grabbed you!" Dad looked really terrified now. "Are you okay?"

"I'm fine. She just knocked the wind out of me. But she had such a grip on her, like a robotic hand, that I swear she didn't seem human."

"Time travel is hard enough to believe. Now you're asking me to believe in aliens?" Malcolm wagged a french fry at me like an admonishing finger.

"So maybe she wasn't an alien." I shrugged. "But she was plenty creepy."

"Creepy and beautiful. That I'd like to see." Malcolm dipped the french fry in ketchup and ate it. The weirdness of all this hadn't affected his appetite at all, though I could barely choke down a crumb.

"This is all really strange. Mom trying to change history—which she shouldn't. Another time traveler attacking you—which she really shouldn't. What's going on?" Dad hadn't touched any of his french fries. Like me, he was too freaked out to eat.

"Maybe the rules have changed. Maybe Mom knows

something the other time-travelers don't. All I know is she's scared and this is important to her." I looked at Dad. "We have to trust Mom, don't we? You said we did."

Dad didn't answer right away. Then he said slowly, "Of course we do." He rubbed his temples the way he does when a crossword puzzle really has him stumped. "You're right. So what is it Mom is trying to do? What does she want you to do?"

"According to Mom and her supposed friend, Morton, we need to do something to clear Dreyfus's name. The military has to admit their mistake and punish the real traitor, Esterházy. But that hadn't happened when I left. Just the opposite. They were protecting him to cover their own butts. I couldn't believe they'd go that far, but they did."

"Sounds like a great conspiracy theory," said Malcolm. "Is this for real? You're trying to prove the military framed Dreyfus? That's like trying to prove the CIA was behind the Kennedy assassination."

"Come on, Malcolm, be helpful here," Dad reproached him, then turned to me. "So you need to uncover the conspiracy?"

"I don't really know. At first I was supposed to get Degas to like Jews so he'd support Dreyfus, but that didn't work. Then I thought maybe I could get Henry to confess or something. I think he's the guy who forged papers to prove Dreyfus's guilt. But I couldn't get close to him."

"This all sounds totally ridiculous!" Malcolm said. "You met Degas and tried to make him like Jews? What were you supposed to do, sell him on the merits of bagels?"

The way Malcolm said it, it did sound silly. But when Mom asked for it, somehow it made sense. How could I explain that?

"Do you know what Mom was doing?" asked Dad.

"Something to do with Zola, this writer guy. I'm guessing she was trying to get him to write something, but I don't know what."

Malcolm shook his head. "Admitting that what you say is true, why would you be the one to time-travel? I'd be so much better at it than you! You don't know history. You don't even know who this 'Zola guy,' as you call him, is."

"I didn't ask for this!" I blinked back tears. No way would I let Malcolm know how much he'd hurt me. Because it was true. He'd be much better at figuring out this stuff than me.

"Sounds like we need to do some research," Dad said, changing the subject. "I've heard the name 'Dreyfus,' but I don't know anything about him really. Maybe we'll find something that will help you or Mom. If you can get back to her."

It seemed like a pretty big if.

While normal tourists went to the Louvre or the Picasso Museum, we went to an Internet café. Wikipedia at last! Once

Dad showed me how to hunt and peck my way around the strange French keyboard, I read about Esterházy, Dreyfus, Henry, Picquart. Every name I'd overheard. Malcolm actually tried to help, reading to me about the start of Zionism, which some historians think had its roots in the Dreyfus affair.

When Theodor Herzl, a Jewish journalist working in Paris, saw the crowd's ugly response to Dreyfus, he developed his theory of Zionism—that assimilation didn't work and Jews could only be safe in their own country. He wrote a book called *The Jewish State* in 1896 proposing this solution to the age-old Jewish problem. Zionism was already in the air then, and I'd had no idea.

Well, really, why should I? I only traveled to very specific snippets of time and had no bigger sense of history than I did here and now, in 2012 Paris. The only way to see history clearly is when it's all in the past and you're looking at it from a distance. You can't figure much out when you're right in the middle of it because it's all too confusing.

But listening to Malcolm, I had some inkling of what Mom meant in her letter—that small events that seem unimportant can turn out to be really important later on. So Dreyfus's unjust conviction led to the weakening of the French military state, led to the collapse of the government, led to intolerance in Europe, which somehow would lead to whatever she's so scared of.

It was too much to think about! What was I supposed to do? I was just one person, and like Malcolm said, not even the right one.

"You should go," I told him, "not me. You'd be so much better at this. I never figure out the right thing to do in time. I don't know the history well enough. I don't know who all these people are." I stopped clicking on websites and put my head down on my arms.

"Hey, you haven't figured it out yet, but you will." Malcolm patted my back in an awkward brotherly way that felt like being pawed by a clumsy bear. "If I could time-travel, I would, but it seems like you inherited the lucky gene. The least I can do is help you while you're here so when you go back, you'll be better prepared. Then it's a little bit like I'm going with you."

"So now that you've read about all this, what do you think I'm supposed to do?" I asked hopefully. "What would *you* do?"

Malcolm chewed on his thumbnail, which is something he does when he's thinking hard about something. "Maybe you could prove that Esterházy's the real traitor. You heard that there was another message between him and the German attaché. What if you found a newspaper reporter who would follow that story? That's the kind of thing you could do, be a deep-throat source to a daring reporter."

"So find me that reporter. Tell me who I should talk to. Help me figure this out."

"It's Zola," Dad said. "That's why your mom had to talk to him. And maybe you do too."

"Dad, Zola writes books! He doesn't work for a newspaper, and he really doesn't like being told what to write." I knew at least that much.

"That's why his writing will be even more powerful, more compelling than any reporter's." Dad leaned forward, serious and intense. "He could finally turn the tide so that the public supports Dreyfus and realizes how corrupt the military has been. Like Malcolm said, it's the press that rights the worst wrongs. It can let the public know the truth about how they've been lied to and fooled by the powerful and wealthy. Without the truth, there's no hope. You've got to get the truth out there."

That was a pretty tall order for one girl.

July 2

I've stayed with Dad and Malcolm for two days now so maybe I won't be able to time-travel anymore anyway. Malcolm wanted to go to the Jewish Museum and do more research, but I needed a break.

"Can we do one single ordinary, fun thing this trip?" I begged.

"We went to Notre Dame!" Malcolm said.

"Yeah, and look what that started. C'mon, Dad, please. You wanted to take photos of the Eiffel Tower, didn't you? Can we go there?"

"Great idea," Dad agreed. "We can go to the Jewish Museum afterward. Okay, Malcolm?"

So we both got what we wanted. It was a clear, sunny day with a brilliant blue sky, the perfect day for Dad to take pictures. After seeing the Eiffel Tower when it was new, it was funny to see it the modern way, like the backdrop for every movie you've ever seen about Paris. A long line of people snaked around the base, waiting to take the elevator to the top.

"I'll stand in line while you take pictures so by the time you're done, we'll be near the front," Malcolm offered.

"Good idea," Dad said. "You want to wait with him?" he asked me.

"After I look around."

"You're not fooling anybody," Malcolm teased. "You're going to draw, aren't you? You think we don't notice that sketchbook you carry everywhere?"

"It's just for notes and doodling," I insisted, "So I'll remember stuff. Anyway who wants to rush to stand in a line? That's your job."

Malcolm stuck out his tongue, but I knew he really didn't mind. He found crowds entertaining. He loved to eavesdrop on strangers' conversations and imagine what their lives were like, so long lines didn't grate on him the way they did on most people.

I tilted my head back, staring into the steel girders crisscrossing their way to the top. Degas saw you being built, I thought. And Claude too. I bet Claude hated me now, after I'd left him just the way he'd begged me not to. I hadn't said anything about him to Dad and Malcolm because really he wasn't part of my job. He was an incidental detail. But a detail that had almost kissed me, and looking up at the Tower, feeling a warm breeze play with my hair, I could almost imagine him standing next to me, his hand gentle on my back.

I threaded my way through the crowds where men hawked flapping toys, squeaking toys, and squishy blobs for toys. There were dozens of different vendors, and they all had the same cheap trinkets, including, of course, bucket-loads of mini Eiffel Towers of every size from key chain to statuette. I definitely wasn't in nineteenth-century Paris anymore. It was more like twenty-first-century Disneyland.

Trying to avoid the man bellowing, "Get your picture taken holding up the Eiffel Tower," I walked behind one of the massive piers. Almost hidden by bushes, there was a brick pillar that looked like an old chimney. It was like a sliver of the nineteenth century in the midst of everything else. A strange throbbing pulsed from it, a weird magnetic pull. Was that what a touchstone felt like? I wondered. Was I finally learning how to recognize one?

I pushed aside a branch, reached into the darkness, and touched the cool stone. A sharp jolt went through me as the seasons furled past, the days and nights wheeled around me, and the mist cleared.

The crowds were gone. So were Dad and Malcolm. I took a deep breath and smelled the nineteenth century.

November 16, 1897

I knew the date from a copy of *Le Figaro* that I picked up. And I knew why I was here, since the newspaper had a letter to the editor that listed all the proofs of Esterházy's guilt, all the reasons Dreyfus was innocent. So the truth was finally out, like Malcolm said it needed to be. Only the letter wasn't written by Zola, the way I expected, but by Mathieu Dreyfus, Dreyfus's brother. Did that mean Zola still needed to be convinced to write his own story, or did I have a totally new job to do? I hated how goals kept shifting. Time travel was like building on sand— nothing stayed the same.

I wondered where Mom was, what she was doing. And where was Morton? If I ever saw him again, I knew better questions to ask him now.

I wasn't sure what else to do so I headed toward the café Nouvelle Athènes, around the corner from Degas's house. It took me a couple of hours, but the day wasn't too cold, just crisp enough, and the light was that golden autumn color that turned everything brilliant and jewel-like. The streets were thick with trees, vines cloaked the houses, and everything felt smaller and cozier after the cold formality of modern Paris. I felt like I was walking through a dream, passing people who looked familiar but weren't, searching faces to find Mom or Claude or Mary Cassatt, somebody I knew. At least I felt like I was doing something, even if all I ended up with were tired feet.

By the time I got to the café, I was hungry and tired. I sat down at one of the little round tables and ordered a hot choco-late, forgetting that I didn't have any money. Before the waiter could come back with the drink I couldn't pay for, I ducked out in a panic. And bumped right into Claude, just like I had that first time. For a second I wondered if he was some kind of touchstone.

He was handsomer than ever, while I looked flustered and sweaty and miserably way too young for him. Anyway, he hated me now because I'd treated him so terribly, leaving him twice without any explanation, even if I hadn't meant to.

"Pardon, Mademoiselle," he said formally as if we were strangers.

"Claude," I said. "It's me, Mira, and you must think I'm horribly rude and there's really no explanation. You just have to trust that I'm not a bad person, and I really want to be your friend."

"Ah, Mira," he said slowly and so coldly the words had icicles hanging from them.

"How is Degas? And Mary Cassatt? And you, your own painting?" I was extra warm and friendly to make up for his remoteness.

"I really cannot stop to chat. My wife is expecting me."

I blinked, trying to keep my face from crumpling. He was married? I gaped at his back, wiping away the tears I couldn't stop as he strode quickly away, not turning to look at me once. What a jerk I was! How could I expect anything to ever happen between us? Of course he got married. Of course I meant nothing to him. Of course.

It's one thing to know something rationally, in your head, and another to feel it in your gut. So I knew I should be fine with Claude living his own life lah-di-da without thinking of me. But it felt like a sharp kick in the stomach. It was a stabbing reminder that this wasn't my time, this wasn't my life. These people weren't my friends and they never could be.

I was here for one reason—to get Mom out of here, to do the job she wanted done so we could both go home. I swallowed the lump in my throat and went to Degas's house. He could tell me where to find Zola, where I might find Mom too.

The servant let me in to the drawing room and went to fetch tea. I hoped that meant some biscuits or cake or toast as well. Because though I thought my heart was breaking, my stomach was making the most noise.

Degas walked in, older than ever, hunched over now like a grandfather. His whiskers were white and his eyes looked clouded over. But he saw clearly enough to recognize me.

"It's Mira, isn't it," he said in his lovely accented English, his voice light and dry. "Enchanting to see you again after all this time. Please do make yourself comfortable and tell me another American phrase as wonderful as turkey buzzard."

"Bologna?" I suggested. "Macaroni and cheese? Tuna casserole?" I was so hungry that all I could think of was food.

Degas frowned. "No, those have none of the flavor of the delightful turkey buzzard. But I will offer you tea all the same."

"Thank you! You've always been so kind to me."

The servant came in with a tray holding teacups, a teapot, slices of bread, and some small cakes. My stomach growled so loudly that I was afraid Degas could hear it.

"You're American, so I almost forgot to ask, but I'm afraid I must do so now," Degas said as he poured the steaming tea into two cups.

"Ask what?" I said as I took my cup and reached for a cake.

"I'm sorry, but these are hard times and I only allow visitors who are anti-Dreyfus. So tell me, are you for or against the traitor?"

"You ask everyone this?" I dropped the cake back onto the tray. Dreyfus had barely been a topic of conversation the last time I was here. "Does it matter that much?"

"I'm afraid it does, yes, very much so. I fought for France in the Prussian War. I believed in France then, and I believe in her now."

"My country, right or wrong?"

"France has done nothing wrong here! From your tone, I take it you're one of those Dreyfusards. I'm sorry to see it, Mira." He shook his head sadly.

"What if the military is wrong? What if an officer faked the evidence that convicted Dreyfus? What if they're protecting the real traitor? How is it patriotic to support that?"

"I think it's time you left." The words were pure ice, and a stony coldness had taken over Degas's face, so kind just minutes before. He sat up stiffly, glaring at me.

I obviously wasn't convincing him of the merits of Jews. My cheeks flamed with anger and something else. Humiliation, that's what I felt, crushed by his cutting certainty. I left Degas to his lonely tea and hoped that Mary Cassatt wouldn't have a Dreyfus litmus test.

She didn't. She was surprised to see me but welcoming all the same. When I told her about Degas, she not only invited me to stay with her usual generosity, she also offered me lunch and the latest news.

"Degas has lost all his friends over this Dreyfus question, you know. Even the Halévy family."

"But he used to eat dinner there once or twice a week! He vacationed with them! Mrs. Halévy developed his photographs for him. He considered the boys to be practically his children." I was astonished.

"Used to." Mary passed me the basket of bread. "Now he won't even hire models if they're Jewish. He threw Claude out, fought with all his artist friends. I think the only one who sees him now is Renoir, sweet, loyal Renoir."

"Aren't you surprised?" I asked. "I thought Degas really cared about his friends. They're like his family. Is he really against the Jews that much?" I felt queasy thinking about it. Anti-Semitism had always been abstract to me, a hatred that belonged to the past, but here it was right in my face.

"Yes and no. Degas is old school, old money, and old family, and the traditional, conservative ways have a deep hold on him. As for Jews, they're just a scapegoat for problems with the government. If Dreyfus weren't Jewish, Degas would still be against him because being for him means believing that the military is corrupt and that the government cares more about its image than finding the real traitor."

"Which it does!" I exclaimed, bolting down a generous hunk of cheese on a slab of bread.

"But this isn't just Degas. The Dreyfus affair is splitting

families apart. People feel passionately both ways. I have to say I can't recall ever seeing anything fire up the public imagination the way this case has. And it's been going on for years!"

"What about Zola?" I asked. "Where does he stand?"

"Zola?" Mary looked like I'd just asked her if she'd invited a cat for dinner. "Why Zola? I didn't know you were friends."

"We're not really. I just wondered. I mean, he's a famous writer so his opinion would matter, wouldn't it?"

"I suppose so. He travels a lot, though. I know he was in Rome when Dreyfus was court-martialed, and he just got back from a few weeks in London."

"Are you friends? I remember you meeting with him at the Café Nouvelle Athènes years ago. He seemed interesting."

Mary wrinkled her forehead, concentrating. "There was a group of us, no? I wouldn't call him a friend, more of an acquaintance, someone everyone in my circle knows, though I personally don't know him well." She turned toward the bookshelf behind her. "And of course I've read his books. Though he hasn't written anything I've truly liked since *Germinal*. You can borrow it if you like."

Mary handed me a green cloth-bound copy of *Germinal*, the title written in elegant gold script. I'd never seen a book that was such a beautiful object, so appealing in its thingness. Unfortunately, it was in French, so not much good to me in its bookness.

"If I could read French better, I'd love to," I said, embarrassed that in all the times I'd visited Mary, my French hadn't improved. For me, it was a matter of days. For her, these visits happened over stretches of years. She'd think I would have improved at least a little unless I was a complete idiot. Which it seemed like I was.

November 23, 1897

I meant to go see Zola. Instead I went to Giverny with Mary to visit her friend, Claude Monet. I should have stayed in Paris and tried to talk to Zola, but since Mary was closing up her house for a week of thorough cleaning, I didn't really have a choice.

And actually, I was glad to go. Giverny was beautiful. The gardens were just like the paintings I'd seen of them in the Museum of Modern Art. Winding paths, graceful willows, ponds full of water lilies, croaking frogs, and humming dragonflies created a fairy-tale world. I could pretend to be a real artist, sketching for hours like everyone else.

Presiding over it all was Monet, with his long white beard, bushy white eyebrows, and friendly warmth. He was the opposite of Degas, sweet and gentle and always outside painting, even in the cold.

The house was full of guests. Besides me and Mary, a couple of writers (neither was Zola), a sculptor named Rodin, and Renoir, who I recognized. And of Monet's eight children, six still lived at home or were there for a visit. All the noise and laughter was the opposite of Degas's Spartan bachelor life. Knowing how he detested Monet and his easygoing good nature, I almost felt like a traitor being there, but it was so nice to spend hours drawing, part of a warm circle of friends and family.

I missed my own family and the circle we'd had. Where was Mom anyway? What were Malcolm and Dad doing right now? I imagined them frozen by the Eiffel Tower, waiting for me to return, the way they had on the walkway of Notre Dame. For me, days had passed. For them, maybe not even a minute, certainly not long enough to miss me. For them it was hot summer; for me it was chilly autumn.

In late afternoons when the light was too dull to paint by, everyone gathered in the large front room in front of the fireplace, sipping tea and eating sweets. There'd been some gossip about Degas, how lonely he was in his self-imposed anti-Dreyfus bubble, but most of the talk was about the Dreyfus case itself. There were so many twists and turns that it was like an elaborate murder mystery.

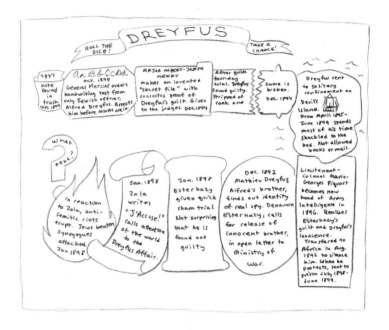

"Look at today's newspaper," Monet said last night. "Zola has entered the discussion. He wrote an essay, not so much about Dreyfus as about Senator Scheurer-Kestner who has seen the evidence of Esterházy's guilt and denounced him as the true traitor."

"May I see?" I tried not to snatch the paper, but reached for it politely. Even with my limited French, I could tell it was expressive writing, not a dry list of facts, but a call to arms. Zola didn't say much, but he ended with: "The truth is on the march and nothing shall stop it." I hoped he was right.

"Will this make a difference?" I asked. This was what Mom had wanted, what she'd worked so hard for, but was it enough? And it was exactly what Dad and Malcolm said needed to happen—the press had to tell the truth so the people would know what the military had done. But would people care?

Monet shrugged. "If the truth is truly on the march, it will. Me, I put my faith in my garden, my paints, and my brushes. To trust the government to do the right thing when it would be such an embarrassing scandal? I have my doubts."

"I wish the whole ugly affair were over," Renoir said. "And Degas could let go of all this, admit he's wrong once the military has admitted they were wrong, and then we could all be friends again."

"Degas holds grudges," Mary said, nibbling at a tart. "I wouldn't count on it. He can be the most loyal, generous friend, but stronger than that is his stubbornness."

"Good for him!" Rodin bellowed. He was a big bear of a man with hands as big as dinner plates and a booming voice

to match. "The man has the courage of his convictions. He stands up for what he believes in. I may not share his beliefs, but I share his backbone! There are too many whiners with small, petty concerns bringing this country down.

"I told you about the criticism the boorish mayor of Calais had about my sculpture of the burghers. Here I am, creating a monumental group of men surrendering the keys to the city—surrendering, I say—and the mayor snipes that I've made their faces too anguished, their attitudes too dejected. The moron wants stoic heroes drained of blood on display, I tell you!"

"Stop complaining, Rodin." Monet smiled. "You love the controversy. Admit it. Otherwise you wouldn't be making that large portrait of Balzac nude. You know how tongues will wag!"

"It's only the study, the model, that's nude. He'll be wearing an impressive cloak in the finished piece."

"But he'll be naked under that, and everyone will know!" Renoir chuckled.

I didn't know who Balzac was, though the name alone sounded heavy with importance. Funny, I thought, Renoir, Degas, Monet, they all sounded light and bubbly, full of sun and warmth. But Rodin and Balzac sounded heavy and hollow. And Dreyfus, Dreyfus sounded like trouble, like a difficult problem I had to solve.

November 24, 1897

Back in Paris on my way home to Mary's, I recognized Degas on the other side of the street, walking aimlessly. He bumped into a man who obviously knew him, but Degas squinted at him as if he couldn't see clearly.

"It's my eyes. You must forgive me, I can't see a thing," he said.

"I'm so sorry to hear that," the friend said.

"I'm used to it." Degas waved away any sympathy. He pulled out his pocket watch, checked the time, and said he had to be going or he would be late.

The other man believed the little charade but I almost laughed. How bad could Degas's eyes be if he could see the small watch face clearly? I couldn't help still liking him. Seeing him alone on the street after spending time with Monet and his crowded household, I felt sorry for Degas's narrow-mindedness, his aristocratic blinders. He was still a great painter and a kind, gentle soul at heart, although he was wrapped in a gruff exterior, armored with stubbornness.

Besides, patriotism cloaks a multitude of sins. He wasn't the first or the last to say, "My country, right or wrong," even when that country was obviously, clearly, blatantly wrong. And

Rodin had a point. It wasn't as if Degas was taking the easy way out. He was miserable in his loneliness; I was sure of it. But he had to follow what he believed. There was something admirable about that.

But of course, being Jewish and automatically suspicious to him now, I couldn't say any of this to Degas. And that wasn't my job anymore. I figured the best place to start was Zola.

Mary Cassatt didn't know him well, but she found out where he lived, not far from the Gare Saint-Lazare. I had it all planned out. I would tell him I was an American journalist and I wanted to interview him about his opinion on the Dreyfus case. If I told him how important his words were, what a difference he was making in international circles, maybe he'd write more, do something to directly support Dreyfus and get the truth out there.

At least that was my plan. Plan B was that maybe he'd tell me where to find Mom. Because I was sure he knew her.

Zola turned out to be absolutely gallant and charming. His cool gray eyes shone with good humor and wit. He was the opposite of big, gruff Rodin—small and neat with elegant fingers. His rooms were like him, orderly and clean, each Chinese vase and glass paperweight clearly in its proper place.

He was so welcoming that I just plunged in and asked him if he could think of a way to support Dreyfus and convince the public of the enormous fraud the military was committing.

"I already wrote an article on the whole sorry affair." Zola gestured to a copy of the article on the table between us.

"Yes, but it's not enough. You wrote about the senator and his stand for the truth. You need to do more than that—to spell out each way the army framed Dreyfus. You need to be dramatic to change public opinion."

"I really think that kind of impassioned argument is best left for the young, someone like you, for example."

"But you have a reputation as a great man of letters. Your opinion matters! Mine is worth nothing. And you wrote that novel criticizing the army before. You have a reputation of not being beholden to anyone."

Zola sighed. "I have a lot more to lose now than I did then."

"But aren't you as passionate about the truth as ever?" I pressed.

"I admit I have been talking to senators, to officers in the army, and what I'm learning is enough to goad even a silent stone into screaming the truth."

"Then you'll do it?"

"I didn't say that." Zola shook his head. "Someone younger really should. Someone who isn't a member of the Legion of Honor. Someone who has less to lose."

I hated to think that I would be less idealistic when I got older, that I'd care less about horrible injustice. I promised myself I wouldn't, that I'd always care about the truth, even if it came with a high cost. Maybe I just had to make Zola realize how awful it all really was.

A man was chained to a bed in a stifling prison, far from his family, not allowed visits or letters or anything that would give him hope. And meanwhile, the real traitor was free to go where he wanted. And the military not only knew he was the actual spy, but they were shielding him from any suspicion. How could anybody with a shred of moral sense stay silent if they knew that? And suddenly I understood that was what Zola had to write about. That was the important truth that needed to be told.

"You know that the army has been protecting Esterházy, the real spy?" I asked, dropping my little bomb.

"Ah, that's something I didn't know!" Zola's eyes lit up. "The corruption goes that far? Do you have names you can give me? What evidence do you have?" He leaned forward eagerly, grabbing a block of paper and fountain pen from his desk. Had I really convinced him?

I described the meeting with Esterházy, but the only name I knew for sure was Henry's.

"Describe the other two men in more detail, the ones wearing the disguises," urged Zola. "I may be able to recognize them."

"Maybe it would be better if show you the sketches I made of them," I suggested. This wasn't about art, but identity, so I tried not to be embarrassed by my unskilled drawing.

"Yes, please do!" Zola leaned forward eagerly as I handed him my sketchbook.

"I don't believe it!" he gasped, recognizing one of the men instantly. "Your bearded man is Major Du Paty, the scoundrel! He's the one who insisted Dreyfus's handwriting matched the treacherous note in the first place. He never cared about finding the real culprit. He was so eager to tar a Jew."

"And the other man?"

Zola examined my sketch again. "That looks very much like Félix Gribelin, the military archivist who was involved in Dreyfus's arrest. Both of these men need Dreyfus to stay guilty."

"So much that they need to protect the real traitor?" I asked. "I can't believe that instead of going after the real spy, the actual danger, they'd rather ruin an innocent man's life. It seems so stupid!"

Zola nodded. "I knew that the conspiracy to convict Dreyfus went to the highest levels of the army, all who knew, absolutely knew, that Dreyfus was innocent, but as you say, they preferred to send an innocent man to Devil's Island rather than admit their ineptitude at first and their responsibility for a cover-up later. But now you're saying it's even worse than that—they not only knew of Esterházy's guilt, they are protecting him!"

"All because Dreyfus was Jewish?" I asked, as if I didn't already know it.

"Yes." Zola sighed. "I thought more of my country, but I was wrong. I wonder if such a thing could have happened in England or in your own America."

It probably could. We weren't such a nice country either. How were we treating African Americans in the 1890s? Or Native Americans? Nobody said anything about that. No important, exciting news stories declaring that justice was on the march. That wouldn't happen until the 1960s!

"It's horrible how much hatred and prejudice can blind people to the truth." Zola went on. "They see what they want to see, even when doing so puts their own interests at risk."

"All that because of a different religion." I felt sick to my stomach.

"Well, more than a religion. It's a racial question, you know.

The 'evil' Jewish race has been a scapegoat for thousands of years. It's easier to hate the other than to tolerate it."

I hadn't thought of Judaism as a racial thing. Sure, it was more than a religion. I'd always considered it a cultural identity, but it was weird to think I'd be judged as a distinctive race. Strange to think that even in the multicultural twenty-first century, racial differences were still used to stereotype people. I wondered what truths we weren't seeing because of racial blinders, what mistakes were being made. Were we any better that the nineteenth-century French?

It was getting late, but I still had to ask about Mom. "This might sound odd," I began, "but I'm looking for a fellow American, an older woman, who is also following this story. Perhaps you know her?"

"Do you mean Serena Goldin?"

Mom! Yes, he knew Mom!

"I saw Madame Goldin just last week. She helped me with the material for my article. I don't know how she got it, but she had some powerful evidence. As you have. I could not write as strong an argument without the two of you, so I'm truly grateful."

I blushed. Was he definitely going to write the article then? Had I really helped him? And, most importantly, where was Mom now? "Do you know where I could find her?" I asked.

"We were actually supposed to meet today, but she never

came. You can try her at her hotel. She stays at L'Américaine on the Boulevard Richelieu."

I tried to stay calm as I thanked Zola and headed down the stairs to the front door. I walked out into the dusk, not sure which way to go. The gaslights were just being lit and the street was full of shadows. But one shadow, there by the side of Zola's house, looked creepily familiar. It was Madame Lefoutre! She was talking to a chimney sweep. I flattened myself to the wall, hoping she hadn't seen me.

The chimney sweep nodded and left. Madame walked in front of me and kept going. This was my chance to see what she was up to. I tried to follow her as discreetly as I could, but she walked quickly and I had to jog sometimes to keep up. Movies make tailing someone look easy, but really it was hard. Where there were a lot of people around, it was easier, but there were empty stretches where all Madame had to do was turn around and she'd see me.

She'd walked about twenty minutes when she did exactly that. She turned to face me, and I swear her eyes glowed a demonic red. Her mouth twisted in an ugly grimace, scarring her perfect face. Her eyebrows swooped down into a menacing glare.

"You!" she hissed.

I stood there frozen in terror. I didn't know what to say or do. She took a step toward me. I stepped back. This time I

didn't have a parasol to whack her with. I
looked around for any kind of weapon;
even a stone would do. But there wasn't
anything. Unless I hit her over the head
with my sketchbook.

"You've ruined everything!" she screeched.
"But it's not over yet, not by a long shot." She
turned, stiff skirts swishing, and strode away. I started following her again, not bothering to be careful now that she knew I
was there.

"Good thing time is on my side!" she yelled. "Now go home
and stop meddling!" She reached out to a bronze fountain.

"What do you mean?" I yelled. But it was too late. She was
gone in a crackling of light.

January 13, 1898

It took a while to find the hotel Zola mentioned, but Serena Goldin had already checked out. Was Mom still here or somewhere else, some *when* else, completely? Or had Madame Lefoutre found her and done something to her? I wished I could get back to Dad and Malcolm and get their help. I touched every fountain and sculpture I passed, but I was still stuck in this time.

At least Zola wrote the article. It came out today, with the big bold headline blaring "J'Accuse!" or "I Accuse!" It sounded better in French than in English, but either way, it was a finger pointing directly at the corruption of the military and those in the government who had helped with the cover-up.

In the article, written as a letter to the president of the French Republic, Zola laid out clearly how the military had rushed to accuse Dreyfus since he was Jewish, and how, once he'd been blamed, they couldn't go back even when his innocence was clear and so was Esterházy's guilt. The honor and image of the military was more important than one man's torture. And having chosen that deal with the devil, the military also punished anyone who got in the way.

WHAT THE ARMY KNEW

Marquis du Paty de Clam

Officer of the Judiciary Police. Suspects Dreyfus as a spy immediately because he's Jewish. Protects Esterhazy once truth is known.

General Auguste Mercier Minister of War.

Arrests Dreyfus for having the same handwriting as the traitor before handwriting tests results are even known. Experts disagree in the end, but lack of proof doesn't matter.

Major Hubert Joseph Henry

Gives false testimony at Dreyfus's trial and creates forged documents to strengthen the case against him. When the truth finally comes out in 1898, he confesses to the forgery and cuts his own throat while in prison. Becomes a hero to military supporters who erect a statue in his honor.

Lieutenant-Colonel Marie-Georges Picquart

As soon as he's appointed Head of Counter-Intelligence in 1895, he grows suspicious of Esterhazy. When he realizes Esterhazy is the actual traitor and Dreyfus is innocent, he reports discovery to senior officers and is sent to Africa to get him quietly out of the way. Back in Paris a year later, he denounces Esterhazy again and is himself sent to prison for a year as punishment.

General Charles-Arthur Gonse

He refuses to listen to Picquart's evidence. Instead, he arranges for Esterhazy's protection and acquittal. He insists on Dreyfus's guilt his whole life.

After showing how corrupt the military had been, Zola wrote a rousing call for justice. I copied it (with thanks to Mary Cassatt for her expert translation).

"It is a crime to lead public opinion astray, to manipulate

it for a death-dealing purpose. It is a crime to poison the minds of the humble, ordinary people, to whip reactionary and intolerant passions into a frenzy while sheltering behind the odious bastion of anti-Semitism. France, the great and liberal cradle of the rights of man, will die of anti-Semitism if it is not cured of it. It is a crime to play on patriotism to further the aims of hatred."

Then he ended just the way Malcolm wanted him to:

"I have but one goal: that light be shed, in the name of mankind which has suffered so much and has the right to happiness. Let them dare to summon me before a court of law! Let the inquiry be held in broad daylight! I am waiting."

Dad once told me about the Watergate hearings, which happened when he was in high school, how the president of the United States had sent "burglars" into Democratic campaign headquarters so he could know about the competition's plans for the presidential election. The whole country was riveted by the congressional hearings into who had done what when, and how far up the chain of command the blame went.

The buck went all the way to the President, Richard Nixon, who had to resign or face being impeached for his crimes. Dad said that even as a high school student, the first thing he did when he came home from school was turn on the TV to watch the hearings. They were more dramatic than any spy movie he'd ever seen.

That kind of public attention and public uproar was happening in Paris. There were demonstrations for Dreyfus, against Dreyfus, for the military, against the military. Esterházy was burned in effigy before the Hôtel de Ville, the Paris city hall. And so was Dreyfus.

It was exciting, dramatic, and totally scary. I didn't know what I was supposed to do or where Mom was (except not in her hotel). Zola had lit the match. The truth was definitely out there, so why did I need to still be here?

I climbed the stairs to the gargoyle gallery at Notre Dame where this had all begun. Looking down at the city, I could see mobs swirling up and down streets. In one plaza, a man on a box was shouting slogans to a crowd around him. In another, piles of newspapers and books were burning, Zola's accusations turned to ash and smoke.

Was this what was supposed to happen? I wished Mom was here, that she could tell me it was all right, and she'd be home soon. It didn't feel right. In fact, it all felt very wrong.

The gargoyles looked down blankly on the frenzied streets. They'd seen much worse, I bet, including the French Revolution when people were guillotined in the public squares, something much more brutal than a pyre of newspapers. The sharp-beaked gargoyle eating the chicken creature still creeped me out, but I couldn't stop myself from reaching out to touch its head.

July 4

And just like then, the world buzzed with a strange staticky sound, the days and nights whirled around me, and I was back where I'd begun this whole weird trip—in 2012. Or if not that exact year, modern times, because looking down from the gallery, I could see that the streets were clogged with cars and buses, streams of tourists, and the occasional bicyclist fighting their way through. Were all the gargoyles touchstones? I was afraid to even brush against one, now that I was back in the time where I belonged. I skirted past an enormous German and plunged down the stairwell, eager to get back to my family.

Where were Dad and Malcolm, though? Were they back at the Eiffel Tower where I'd left them?

Since the hotel was close by, I decided to check there first.

The good news was that not only did we still have rooms there (the right time!), but Dad and Malcolm were actually in them.

"Mira!" Dad hugged me. "Where were you? What happened to you?"

"So this time you noticed me going?" I asked.

"Of course we noticed! We looked for you everywhere! We came back here thinking you'd find us, rather than the other way around."

"And that worked," I said, suddenly exhausted, plopping down on the bed.

"So where were you? Where's Mom?"

I wished I had the answers Dad wanted, but I didn't.

"Does that mean she didn't succeed? She didn't do what she needed to?" Malcolm asked. He didn't add "and you didn't do it either," but I knew he was thinking it. We all were.

"Zola wrote the story Mom wanted," I said. "But maybe it didn't make the difference she thought it would. I wasn't there long enough to know. Did Dreyfus get a second trial? Was his name cleared? Was Esterházy ever convicted? And what about all the officers who framed him and covered up the truth?"

Dad looked at Malcolm. "Do you know what happened to Dreyfus?"

"And what about Zola?" I asked. "Why did he expect to be put on trial? What was the inquiry he said he was waiting for?"

"I don't know," Malcolm admitted. "We'll have to look

things up again. That's the only way to know if you guys did what you were supposed to do anyway."

We headed for the Internet café again. It didn't seem to matter that we were in Paris, the most romantic city in the world. All we'd seen were Notre Dame and the bottom of the Eiffel Tower. And the Internet café.

"Did you guys go up the Eiffel Tower? Did you get some good photos, Dad?" I hoped they'd had some fun at least.

"I took some decent pictures, but we were looking for you so we lost our place in line. That's okay, we'll do it again, all three of us. Maybe all four of us even," Dad said hopefully.

Maybe all I'd get out of Paris was what I drew in my sketchbook. I let Malcolm look stuff up on Wikipedia while I sketched outside, imagining Claude drawing beside me.

What Malcolm found wasn't happy news. "Dreyfus did have a second trial, but despite the overwhelming evidence of his innocence, he was still found guilty. But because of Zola and the frenzy that his article started, the French president pardoned Dreyfus so he was freed. Wait, there's more…"

"At least you got him off Devil's Island," Dad said. "That's something."

"I didn't do that. Zola did. And it wasn't enough."

"Zola wouldn't have written the story without you."

"You mean without Mom. We both gave him information." I should have felt proud, but I didn't. Not without Mom.

"Dreyfus was finally exonerated," Malcolm said, "but not until 1906! By then, there was a general amnesty clearing anyone in the military who framed him. So they basically got away with it."

"What happened to Zola?" I asked Malcolm, expecting the worst.

"That's not good either." Malcolm squinted at the screen and summarized the bad news, "Zola was tried for libel, and the military, of course, lied again—and again and again. And since Zola wasn't allowed to introduce evidence about the truth of what he wrote—the name of Dreyfus wasn't permitted to be even mentioned—there was no way for him to prove his case. It wasn't a trial, it was a total joke, but the mob hysteria Zola had written about showed up in full force at his trial. He received death threats. Crowds threw rotten vegetables at him, yelling 'Drown the Jews! Long live the army!'" Malcolm turned to look at me. "Were people saying that kind of stuff to you?"

"Only Degas," I said. "Well, not really. But he made it clear he had no use for Jews, so you can see how well I did with that bagel-selling job you recommended."

Anyway, Zola wasn't Jewish, but he'd spoken up for the Jews and that was enough to label him one. He was stripped of his Legion of Honor status and sentenced to the maximum penalty, a year in prison and a fine of 3,000 francs. To escape prison, he fled to London, an exile from his own country. While he was gone, his property was sold by the government to pay the fine.

I felt awful for Zola. I'd convinced him that he should take the risk, and he was punished for it. As was everybody who had tried to help Dreyfus. And what about Mom? Had she been punished too? Had Madame gotten to her? I had to go back and find out. I had to find her.

Malcolm had other ideas. He suggested we go see Zola's grave in the Montmartre Cemetery.

"I didn't know how great the guy was," he said. "Seems like the least we can do is put some flowers on his grave or something. Right, Dad?"

"Sure, and we'll see a different part of Paris too. Montmartre is supposed to be especially charming."

I smiled. "I know that neighborhood pretty well. Let me give you a tour."

So we finally did something like regular tourists. I showed Dad and Malcolm where Degas used to live, Mary Cassatt's and Renoir's homes, the café where everyone hung out.

It was strange seeing all these places in modern times, with cars parked on the paved streets, electric streetlights, parking signs, trash cans, bus stops, all the things that weren't there in the nineteenth century. But some things stayed the same, like the streets themselves.

"You really were here, weren't you?" Malcolm gaped at me. "I mean, you know this neighborhood. You know where you're going."

"Give me a little credit. I may not know history, but I have a pretty good sense of direction."

"It's just hard to really believe it all," Malcolm said. "You met Degas! And Zola!"

"Too bad convincing Zola to write his article wasn't enough."

"Why do you say that?" Dad said. "You made a tremendous difference."

"No," I disagreed. "Because if things were fixed, then Mom would be back with us."

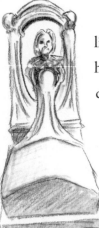

We walked through the cemetery, which was like a little town itself with graves built like small houses and elaborate sculptures. Usually I like cemeteries—I'm weird that way. I find them peaceful and pretty, kind of like gardens for dead people. And although this was an especially nice cemetery, I didn't feel peaceful at all.

"This is it!" Malcolm called, pointing out a bronze bust set into a marbled stage. It was

Zola's grave, magnificent and important, just like the man had been.

"Looks like he got the recognition he deserved in the end," Dad remarked. "This is hardly a shy little nobody's grave."

Malcolm laid the bouquet of bright daisies we'd brought onto the stone under the bust. "I'd like to think I'd stand up for what I believe the way you did," he said to the sculpture.

I wanted to think that too. Would I? Was I brave enough?

There's a Jewish tradition that when you visit someone's grave, you leave a stone on the marker. I found a smooth gray pebble and set it on Zola's tomb. "Thank you," I said. "For Dreyfus and for all Jews. For everybody who believes in justice." I touched the brown marble lightly. "Thank you."

June 11, 1899

I started to say thank you again. I tried to get the words out. But space had collapsed around me, and time whirled by. Zola's grave was a touchstone.

I was still in the Montmartre Cemetery, but the grave was gone, because, of course, Zola was still alive. I had to be back in the nineteenth century; one gulp of air told me that. But when exactly? And did that mean I still had a job to do? Could I find Mom at last?

"There you are!" I heard a screech. It was Madame Lefoutre. She leaped out from behind a stone angel as if she'd just time-traveled herself. Was that possible? Could she chase me through time? I wasn't about to ask. I gathered my skirts (yes, I was in that dress again) and sprinted away from her, not caring where I went so long as it was far from her.

I zigzagged through the streets, turning corners, trying to lose her in the narrow, winding neighborhood. A carriage almost jolted into me; I jostled a bristle-mustached man and nearly ran straight into an old woman walking her poodle. The streets were more crowded now, and I felt safer, like I could stop and catch my breath.

That's when I saw her again. Her back was to me and she hadn't seen me yet, but it was definitely Madame. I turned back around another corner and found myself across the street from Degas's home.

Why not? I thought. At least I'd be safe from Madame. I rang the bell, and the same old servant let me in.

"I'm so sorry to intrude, Monsieur Degas, but I happened to be in the neighborhood…" I tried to smooth my dress into looking decent, and I wiped the sweat off my forehead. At least for once I wasn't lying. I really did just happen to be here.

"Come in, come in. Have a seat. You look like you could use a good cup of tea. Or perhaps something stronger?" Degas was his old, welcoming self. Maybe he was done with measuring everything according to the Dreyfus Affair, yes or no. He'd been without his friends for a long time by now. Whenever now was. Which was actually a good question.

"Thank you, I'd love some tea. And please forgive me my confusion, but I've forgotten today's date."

"You have an appointment you've forgotten?"

"No, I mean I don't remember what day it is."

"Tuesday. Today is Tuesday. You're a bit young to have these lapses, aren't you? It's the kind of thing you'd expect from me." Degas chuckled. "I often forget what hour it is." He took his watch out of his vest pocket and peered at it. "Almost four, so time for tea indeed."

This wasn't helping at all. I tried a different tactic. "Do you have today's newspaper? I haven't had a chance to read it yet."

"Of course." Degas reached for a folded-up journal on the table next to his chair and handed it to me. "You're still interested in that Dreyfus, I imagine. You can see the results of his second trial—guilty again. No surprise there. But that spineless president pardoned the traitor. All the bad press France has been getting intimidated the fool. Bah! Who cares at this point! I'm tired of it all, aren't you?"

I listened with half an ear, trying to read and pay attention at the same time. The date, I noticed, was June 11, 1899, and as Degas had said, the new court had upheld the earlier verdict. Zola had written something about the trial: "There will exist no more detestable monument to human infamy…the ignorance, folly, madness, cruelty, deceit, and crime of the trial will lead tomorrow's generations to tremble with shame." Such stirring words! It was strange to think I'd just been at his tomb. Was he back in France or still in London?

"Aren't you?" Degas repeated, shoving a teacup at me.

"Oh, yes, sorry. I'm a bit distracted." I took a warming sip. "I wish this whole affair would be over. It's gone on for such a long time now."

"Yes, far too long. Weakening the entire government, it is."

"And you, how are you doing? Still collecting art? Still painting?" What a dumb thing to say. Of course he was still doing both, but I didn't want to talk about Dreyfus, not with Degas. What I really wanted to ask was whether he was friends with the Halévys again, whether he'd seen Claude.

"Are we doomed to small talk, my girl? I thought we were far beyond that." Degas gave me a piercing look, and I swear he knew who I really was. But how? That was impossible.

I plastered on a smile, as simpering as I could make it. "I've never been much for deep discussions. You know that. I was just wondering how dear Claude is. Have you seen him lately?"

"He can't be that dear to you, the way you treated him," Degas snapped.

"The way I treated him?" My fingers trembled holding the delicate saucer.

"He was in love with you, and you left him without a word."

My mind went blank, empty of a single plausible lie to explain my sudden disappearances. And I couldn't bear to think of how much I must have hurt Claude.

"I really must be going." I set down my cup, trying to sound calm. Was it really true? Had Claude loved me? What difference did it make? He hated me now. And was married with a nice wife, probably several kids too. And what could I have done to stop that? Absolutely nothing.

"Yes," drawled Degas. "I suppose you must. Always going. It's what you do."

I blushed, miserable. So that was what I was known for—running away. Leaving. And it was true.

"Thank you for the tea. It's good to see you so well." I acted composed while inside every nerve was shaking. I had to get out of there, away from Degas's sharp scrutiny, his harsh judgment, even if it meant running into Madame again.

But the street was empty when I came out. I didn't see her or anybody else I knew all the way to Zola's. Not Mom, not Claude, not anybody.

I had no real reason to go to Zola's except that I didn't know where else to go. He wasn't home, but the maid said she expected him back soon, so I decided to wait. I was poking through the bookshelf when the door opened. It wasn't Zola, though.

It was Madame.

I grabbed an ivory-capped walking stick that was leaning in the corner. Maybe it was one of those kinds that had a blade hidden inside, but even if it wasn't, I could hit her with the stick.

"Calm down, child," Madame Lefoutre commanded. "I'm not going to hurt you. I'm helping you."

"I bet!" I snarled, raising the stick over my head threateningly.

"I'm setting things right. You don't understand what's really going on here. Because of you, poor Mr. Zola here will die. Can you live with that on your conscience?"

"You're lying!"

"Am I? Am I really?" She tilted her chin up, proud and defiant and dangerously beautiful, like some poisonous flower. "Ask your mother. Maybe for once she'll tell you the truth. You have it all wrong. She's the one interfering. I'm cleaning up her messes."

Before I could answer, she turned and left, leaving me with the walking stick over my head when Zola walked in. I quickly leaned it back against the wall. Lucky for me, Zola was much older than the last time I'd seen him, and with his stooped-over, slow shuffle, he didn't notice anything strange. His face was creased with wrinkles, his gray beard chiseled to a point on his chin.

"Ah, Serena, so good to see you again." He kissed the air next to my cheeks. He must have thought I was my mom. I'd always thought we didn't look at all alike, but there had to be some resemblance for Zola to make that mistake.

"I'm sorry, Monsieur Zola, but I'm not Serena. I'm Mira, the American journalist who interviewed you several years ago."

"Of course!" Zola said. "Now sit, please. Colette will bring us something splendid, I'm sure."

"How was London?" I asked.

"Horrible, as you can imagine. Terrible weather, worse food. The only saving grace was that I met Oscar Wilde, just released from jail himself. He told me I should take comfort in my guilty verdict since it's always a mistake to be innocent, while being a criminal takes imagination and courage. And for him, the halo of sin has made him all the more popular in London fashion. He's invited out every night and dines on his witty stories of prison life."

"And you? Are you more popular for your guilty verdict?"

"Alas, no. Only the English appreciate crime that way. The French, it seems, are repulsed by it. Or perhaps it is the nature of our crimes. If I had seduced a young earl like Oscar, that could be forgiven, but to criticize the Grand Army, no, never!"

"If it is hard for you here, perhaps it's best to leave again," I said. Maybe if he left France he wouldn't die as Madame had said he would. I didn't think I would be directly responsible for any harm that might come to him, but since he'd written "J'Accuse," Zola had received plenty of ugly threats from people who considered themselves good patriots. "Italy would be pleasant. Sunny, and you'd eat well."

"I'm too old and tired to be chased out of my home again," Zola grumped.

Looking around at all the Chinese porcelain, the statuettes, including some by Degas, the piles of books and papers, I could understand why the thought of moving was exhausting.

My gaze dropped from the mantelpiece full of precious objects to the fireplace itself. It was caked with soot, and suddenly I remembered that the last time I'd been here, I'd seen Madame talking to a chimney sweep. Had she paid off the chimney sweep to somehow clog the chimney so that Zola would suffocate? When she talked about Zola dying, she meant because of her, not because of me. Anyway, the chimney didn't

look safe and I said so to Zola.

"It's fine. Don't worry. The chimney has been cleaned already this year, as it is every year," said Zola. "Forget about some old soot—I want to know what Americans are saying about Dreyfus, what they think of us French. I fear we are despised as brutes by everyone now." Zola shook his head sadly. "Hard to believe that the country that enshrined the Rights of Man so publicly after the French Revolution could have fallen so low."

We talked about Dreyfus, the press, the furious mobs, the

future of France, but no more mention was made of moving. Or of the chimney.

The light was dimming through the windows. It was time to go, but I was afraid to leave Zola. "I know it's been difficult," I said, "but I want to thank you—for Dreyfus, for France, for all of us. You've spoken out against a monstrous injustice and changed how people think about human rights. You've shown how one person can make a difference."

"You exaggerate!" Zola waved away my words.

"No, it's true. I admire your courage and convictions." I took his hand. "I hope we'll meet again."

"I'm sure we will."

But I was just as certain we wouldn't. Somehow this visit felt final. And really, what more was there to do? Finally, thanks to "J'Accuse," there was broad public support for tolerance and fairness against prejudice and corruption. Wasn't that the change Mom wanted? It was definitely a change I wanted, and I was proud I'd had even a small part in it.

Leaving the house, I glanced up at Zola's roof. Maybe I'd imagined the chimney sweep. Maybe everything would be okay.

I crossed the street, drawn to an odd stone marker I hadn't noticed before. Maybe before it had been unremarkably drab, but now it glowed eerily. Was I supposed to touch it? Even without the glow, it was a strange stone slab with a circular wreath at the top. I read the inscription on it and realized it was meant to mark the Paris Meridian. It had to be part of some kind of astronomical instrument, which made sense if it was a touchstone.

I tried to pull my hand away, but as if moving on its own, it reached out slowly toward the marker. If I left, I wouldn't be able to check on Zola. I wanted to stay, not find a touchstone. But I couldn't help myself. The throbbing stone drew my hand like a magnet. I touched the cool grainy surface. The glow shimmered and deepened, coiling me up in pitch blackness and blinding light, a dizzying whirlpool of time.

July 4

I was back in the cemetery, by Zola's grave. I collapsed on the marble, sobbing.

"I tried to save you, really I did! I'm so sorry!" I wailed.

"What's the matter?" Dad asked. "Who were you trying to save?"

"Zola!" I guessed this time they hadn't noticed I was gone at all, so I explained where I'd been and how I'd left Zola even though Madame might try to kill him. "I thought I'd made a difference, but it wasn't enough—Zola might still die and I didn't bring Mom home."

"Maybe not this time, but next time," Dad said.

"Will there really be a next time?" I asked.

"There has to be a next time, because Mom is still gone. And Madame Lefoutre is still out there."

"Next time, you'll time-travel instead of me, Malcolm," I sniffled. "And I bet you'll be a lot better at it."

Malcolm shrugged. "I think you did great. I couldn't have done better. And it wasn't your job to save Zola. You don't even know if he was killed. But you do know you made a difference for Dreyfus."

Dad put his arm around me. "You did much more than that. You made a difference for all of us. 'J'Accuse' started people thinking about the importance of human rights in a way that hadn't happened before. Maybe you didn't prevent the collapse of the French government and whatever else Mom was afraid of, but you helped Zola strike that match. You helped light a fire that still burns bright."

I smiled, leaning into his familiar smell of shaving cream and cotton. "I guess I did."

We took the metro back to the Marais, but instead of going to our hotel, we made a quick stop at an Internet café. I had to know what happened to Zola.

He died a few years after I'd last seen him, so if Madame was responsible, she didn't kill him right away. But reading how he died, I knew that she had something to do with it. The chimney was blocked, some said by accident, but others thought it was sabotaged by political protestors angry at Zola's defense of Dreyfus. Zola suffocated from carbon monoxide poisoning, and I didn't doubt for a second that it was intentional.

"At least it didn't happen right after I left," I said. "It wasn't my fault."

"No matter when it happened, it wouldn't be your fault," Dad argued. "You're not responsible for other people's actions."

"Even if it was because of the article I encouraged Zola to write?"

"You can't think like that!" Malcolm objected. "If you worry about how crazy people will react when you do the right thing, you'll never do anything! Zola had to write 'J'Accuse.' He had to get people thinking about what kind of government they really wanted, what kind of army."

"Come on," Dad said. "We've spent enough time in Paris in front of computer screens. We still owe Malcolm his choice since we never went there the day of the Eiffel Tower like we said we would."

"Where was that?" I asked.

"The Museum of Jewish Art and History," Malcolm said. "A happy subject for a change, right?"

The museum turned out to be a few blocks from our hotel, housed in an old private mansion. As soon as we walked through the gate into the courtyard, I felt a jolt of recognition. I'd only seen him once, that time at the racetrack. And there had been the horrible caricatures in the newspaper that turned his likeness into a devil. Here he was again, Lieutenant Colonel Alfred Dreyfus, proud in his uniform, holding his broken sword high in a salute through the ages.

"It's Dreyfus," Malcolm said. "You really did help him."

"You did too. We all did it together," I corrected.

"It's good to see him honored after the suffering he endured."
Dad circled the bronze sculpture slowly. "It's good to know that some wrongs can be righted."

I wasn't sure about that. Dreyfus had lost his health and spent four years on Devil's Island, but he died an officer of the Legion of Honor, so at least his reputation, his good name, had been returned to him. The statue was a figure of bravery, of determination. I remembered the words Dreyfus had cried during his ritual degradation when the insignias of his rank were torn from his uniform and his sword snapped in two: "I am innocent!"

The statue seemed to be yelling those words into the sky. It vibrated with an energy, a power, that went beyond art. Was it a touchstone? I didn't want to leave Dad and Malcolm, not yet, but I couldn't help myself. I had to know if Dreyfus would carry me back to his time and to Mom.

I reached out and touched the cool bronze. No crackling of light, no blurring static. Nothing. The statue felt central to me, alive somehow, but it wasn't a touchstone, at least not the time-travel kind. I thought of the dictionary definition of the word.

touchstone: a test or criterion for determining the quality or genuineness of a thing, from an actual stone used to test the purity of gold or silver.

And Dreyfus was definitely that kind of touchstone for me, a test for tolerance, for fighting for justice, for what was right. I wanted to hold on to it tightly, but the things that are the most important won't fit in your hand.

"Let's go into the museum," I said.

"Yeah," said Malcolm. "It's time to be a regular tourist."

And it was, but as we walked back to the hotel a couple of hours later, I could tell Dad was somewhere else. "So the question is," he said, "where should we go next? What part of history do you think Mom will try to change?"

"I haven't got any more letters from her. I have no idea."

I supposed we had to wait for a postcard.

And when we got back to the hotel, one was there for us. From Mom.

Author's Note

This note is for the curious reader who wants to know more about Paris, the Impressionists, Émile Zola, and the Dreyfus Affair. Paris in the 1880s and '90s was a modern city with broad boulevards, wells supplying water, and garbage pickup. Before 1884, rubbish was strewn on the streets in such rancid piles that men took to wearing flowers in their lapels to mask the smell.

Eugene Poubelle, a city administrator, introduced zinc bins to collect trash, which is why a garbage can is "une poubelle" in French. Electric lights were just beginning to be used, as Edgar Degas did in the gallery exhibit he organized. And the Eiffel Tower, built as a temporary structure between 1887 and 1889 for the 1900 World's Fair, proved to be such a popular emblem of French modernism that it still stands today as a major tourist attraction.

The Impressionists

The last Impressionist Exhibition took place in 1886, the same year Zola wrote *The Masterpiece*, his novel based on his friend Paul Cézanne. The exhibit of 1881 was the sixth exhibit, and the last one curated by Degas. I conflated his use of electric lights and colored walls with the 1886 exhibit, when Seurat's *La Grande Jatte* was displayed. Impressionism began in the 1870s as a modern movement of painting actual life, as opposed to the dull, academic, officially recognized art of mythological or historical subjects. Degas was part of the core group, even though he despised *plein air* (open-air) painting, which many Impressionists embraced. Claude Monet, Édouard Manet, Gustave Caillebotte, Camille Pissarro, and Cézanne, and later Paul Gauguin and Vincent Van Gogh, all painted outdoors, trying to capture light and movement as much as their actual subjects. Although ridiculed by the press at first, by the 1890s Impressionism began to be accepted, with the artists selling their paintings for good prices.

The Dreyfus Affair

The outline of the Dreyfus Affair given in this book is all true. It started in 1894 with a cleaning woman who worked as a spy for the French military at the German Embassy in Paris. There she found an incriminating "bordereau" (memorandum) that listed French military capabilities. In October 1894, Captain Alfred Dreyfus was immediately suspected, being the only Jew in the officer corps, and arrested on the slim evidence that the handwriting supposedly matched his. (Conflicting experts disagreed, with the main proponent a vocal anti-Semite.)

Dreyfus was neither told of the charges against him, nor allowed to contact his family or a lawyer. Appalled by how badly Dreyfus was treated, the director of the prison alerted the Minister of War and the Military Governor of Paris, advocating for Dreyfus but to no avail. The military tried to keep the arrest secret, but news of it leaked out.

At that point, the entire military hierarchy jumped on the case, eager to prove their patriotism and root out Jews from the army. Dreyfus's brother, Mathieu, hired Edgar Demange, a noted criminal lawyer, devout Catholic, and strong supporter of the military. Demange agreed to take the case but warned Mathieu that if after examining the evidence, he found it incriminating, he would quit, a signal to all France of Dreyfus's guilt. Mathieu staunchly believed in his brother's innocence and didn't hesitate to take that chance.

Upon reading the file offered by the military, Demange told the family that Dreyfus had been accused solely because he was Jewish. He added, "It is abominable. I have never seen such a dossier. If there is justice, your brother will be acquitted."

The First Dreyfus Trial

The trial lasted three days in November 1894. More than twenty-four witnesses from most of the offices of the military's General Staff testified against Dreyfus. No one from the high command spoke in his defense. Fewer than a dozen of his fellow officers were willing to risk defending him. Still, even the prosecution witnesses were forced to admit under oath that Dreyfus had always acted honorably. One even called him "incapable of treason."

The sole evidence was the supposedly matching, yet not quite matching, handwriting. Alphonse Bertillon, the blatantly anti-Semitic expert witness, offered a convoluted theory to explain that the reason the handwriting wasn't a good match was because Dreyfus had imitated his wife's and brother's handwriting to disguise his own. According to Bertillon, this effort to disguise proved that Dreyfus really had written the bordereau and felt guilty for doing so.

Dreyfus wrote in his diary that the arguments against him were so flimsy and histrionic, the arguments for exoneration so clear and compelling, that he expected to be acquitted just as his lawyer had predicted. However as deliberations began, Commandant Charles du Paty, following the orders of General Auguste Mercier, delivered to the judges a secret dossier of fabricated evidence.

This dossier was created by a counterintelligence agent,

Hubert-Joseph Henry, and attested to Dreyfus having an affair, which he hadn't; being a gambler with enormous debts, which he wasn't; and being loyal to Germany because he spoke German and visited Alsace-Lorraine where he had family. That thousands of other Frenchmen spoke German and lived in Alsace-Lorraine, a territory that had changed hands between France and Germany several times, didn't seem to be a compelling argument against Dreyfus's guilt. Most convincing was a forged letter, supposedly from the Italian attaché, that named Dreyfus as a German spy.

Injustice for Dreyfus

By a unanimous vote, the military tribunal convicted Dreyfus in December 1894. They ordered him to repay the military for the expenses of the trial and sent him to solitary confinement on Devil's Island in French Guyana, off the coast of Brazil. The Ministry of Foreign Affairs was enormously relieved to have gotten through the trial so quickly, having protected national security and avoided igniting tension with Germany. The French press echoed these sentiments, adding with ferocious glee that the menace from the Jews had been quashed. Even the far left despised Dreyfus and felt he deserved the death penalty, which wasn't permitted under French law.

While the French press celebrated the downfall of the evil Jew, the British newspapers called for transparency, insisting the charges were too grave to allow for a secret, closed trial. The rest of the world took little notice of what was happening in Paris. The Dreyfus Affair wasn't an affair yet, but a simple court-martial.

Dreyfus filed an immediate appeal, which was summarily rejected by Commandant du Paty, the same man who had given the judges the fabricated file. Instead Du Paty offered a lighter sentence in exchange for a full list of the information given to the Germans. Given that he knew the charges had been trumped up, it was a cynical offer, one that Dreyfus rejected, proclaiming his innocence.

The public display of Dreyfus literally being stripped of his rank took place on January 6, 1895, in the Morland Courtyard of the War College. The ceremony took place behind iron gates, but hordes of people crowded into the square in front of the college. More thronged onto the nearby roofs and balconies, eager to see the reviled traitor's humiliation.

Thousands of troops lined the courtyard as a military clerk read the verdict. "Alfred Dreyfus, you are unworthy to bear arms. I hereby degrade you in the name of the French people. Let the judgment be executed."

In response, Dreyfus raised his right hand and shouted, "I swear and declare that you are degrading an innocent man. *Vive la France!*"

A drumroll muffled his words as an officer stripped off

Dreyfus's cap and tore the insignia, gold braid, and ornaments off his jacket. As a final insult, the officer took Dreyfus's sword and broke it over his knee. Through it all, Dreyfus held his head high, yelling, "Innocent! I am innocent!"

The crowds inside and outside the War College, both military and public, jeered Dreyfus, calling out, "Down with the Jew! Judas! Traitor! Kill all the Jews!"

As ugly as the ceremony was, it was only the beginning of Dreyfus's suffering. He spent fifteen days locked in a mesh cage on the deck of a ship, exposed to the elements and the insults of the crew, before landing at Devil's Island in French Guyana. In an old leper colony that had been turned into a prison, Dreyfus was chained to his bed for days on end, always in solitary confinement. Unaware of any efforts to prove his innocence, Dreyfus spent four dark years there. In his diary he wrote of his desperation and despair, his loss of faith in justice and reason. Only the thought of his wife and children kept him from committing suicide.

The Real Traitor

Two years after the trial, the same cleaning woman/agent who had found the first bordereau discovered a new document that suggested the original traitor was still actively selling secrets to the Germans. Major Georges Picquart suspected Major Ferdinand Walsin Esterházy, an inveterate gambler, but he found no hard evidence until six months later when he closely examined the document and recognized the famous handwriting from the first bordereau.

Shocked to realize that Esterházy was the original traitor and that Dreyfus must be innocent, Picquart reviewed the secret dossier and realized it held no proof, only hysterical speculation. Horrified by what he'd learned, Picquart went to his superiors, du Paty and Henry, and told them of his discoveries.

The military refused to acknowledge their mistake, instead closing ranks around Esterházy and protecting him. As for Picquart, he was ordered out of Paris and sent to northern Africa where his pangs of conscience wouldn't be heard.

A Brother's Efforts

From the beginning, Mathieu Dreyfus worked tirelessly to clear his brother's name. With the help of the lawyer, Demange, he discovered the contents of the secret dossier. Since repeated petitions for retrials were rejected, Mathieu decided to present his case directly to the public. He approached a Jewish journalist, Bernard Lazare, to write a clear argument exposing the travesty of justice. Mathieu had 35,000 copies of the pamphlet, titled "A Judicial Error," printed in Brussels (to avoid legal action against him for committing libel) and distributed in France.

Lazare wrote about Dreyfus: "He is a soldier, but he is a Jew, and it is as a Jew that he was prosecuted. Because he was a Jew, he was arrested; because he was a Jew, he was tried; because he was a Jew, he was convicted; because he was a Jew, the voice of justice and truth could not be heard in his favor; and the responsibility for the condemnation of that innocent man falls entirely on those who provoked it by their vile exhortations, lies, and slander…They needed their own Jewish traitor to replace the classic Judas, a Jewish traitor they could use every day to cover an entire race with shame…"

In response to this pamphlet, *Le Matin* printed a facsimile of the original bordereau as proof of Dreyfus's guilt. Mathieu seized this opportunity to have posters hung all over the city showing his brother's handwriting next to the bordereau so that anybody could see the two didn't match. In France and abroad, handwriting experts agreed that Dreyfus hadn't written the bordereau.

The Dreyfus Affair Begins

Picquart, back in France in 1897, realized that he had been right about Esterházy and that his superiors had known the truth all along. His transfer to North Africa had been a setup, a form of exile. Recognizing how far the military would go to keep their secrets, Picquart added a codicil to his will that an envelope be delivered to the president of the Republic in case of his death. The envelope contained an accusation against the General Staff of perpetrating a vast cover-up, treating the law with contempt, and knowingly punishing an innocent man.

Finally unable to keep quiet any longer, Picquart told a lawyer friend what he knew. That friend told the vice president of the Senate, a powerful and popular senator, who told the President, Félix Faure, and General Jean-Baptiste Billot, who promised an investigation but did nothing. Still, through Picquart, the wall of secrecy and conspiracy that the military had so carefully built was cracked.

The army, warned that the senator knew the identity of the real traitor, tried to protect Esterházy, but Mathieu's posters with the bordereau caught the eye of a banker, Jacques de Castro, who recognized the handwriting of his sleaziest client, Esterházy. Convinced that his client had to be the real traitor, de Castro gave Mathieu some of Esterházy's letters from his bank files as proof of a real match.

Mathieu gave this proof to the senator and approached the mainstream press, this time *Le Figaro*, writing a letter to the Minister of War that spelled out Esterházy's guilt and demanded justice for Dreyfus. The letter appeared on November 16, 1897, and ignited a fury of interest. The Dreyfus case was now the Dreyfus Affair.

J'Accuse

Émile Zola, the novelist who was so beloved that he'd been inducted into the Legion of Honor in 1892, hadn't paid much attention to Dreyfus. But after reading Mathieu's letter, he wrote his own essay for *Le Figaro*, not focusing on Dreyfus so much as on the senator and his nobility in trying to right a horrible wrong.

A Nation Divided

The renewed interest forced the military to put Esterházy on trial in January 1898. Once again, the judges ruled for a closed session on grounds of national security. The trial lasted two days, the deliberation not even five minutes. Not surprisingly, the military judges voted unanimously to acquit Esterházy. The real traitor left the courtroom to shouts of "Long Live France," "Long Live the Army," and "Death to the Jews!" The senator, Picquart, and Mathieu Dreyfus all testified against Esterházy, only to be threatened by the angry hordes outside.

Esterházy went free. The senator, however, lost his re-election for the post of vice president. Even worse, Picquart was arrested and sent to prison. That same day, January 13, 1898, was when Zola's "J'Accuse" appeared. It became one of the most famous headlines in the history of journalism. With his forceful writing, Zola turned the Dreyfus Affair into an enormous political, military, and social scandal. He held all of France accountable for the grotesque miscarriage of justice, for fanning the ugly flames of anti-Semitism.

In his clear prose, Zola laid out how the General Staff had seized Dreyfus as the culprit because of his Jewishness, and once they'd made the accusation, they couldn't go back. Dreyfus was sacrificed to the integrity of the army in a devil's bargain. One innocent man's torture paid to keep the reputation of the military unstained.

Zola finished the essay with a list of accusations against specific men on the General Staff, naming names even though he knew he risked the charge of libel by doing so. It was a risk he had to take. "I have but one goal: that light be shed, in the name of mankind which has suffered so much and has the right to happiness. My ardent protest is only a cry from my very soul. Let them dare to summon me before a court of law! Let the inquiry be held in broad daylight! I am waiting."

He didn't have to wait long. As soon as the article appeared, his apartment was pelted with stones and excrement. He received death threats, and ugly crowds jeered him when he appeared in public. The official response was as he expected. Three weeks later, his trial for libel was held in the Palais de Justice. Taking longer than either Dreyfus's or Esterházy's trials—ten days— the process involved everyone named in "J'Accuse." The crowds packing the courtroom and spilling outside were bigger and rowdier than those for the two military tribunals.

Unfortunately for Zola, there was no question of justice for him, any more than for Dreyfus. The judges refused to allow any defense that mentioned Dreyfus or actual facts from the Affair, basically making it impossible for Zola to defend himself. The military witnesses, however, were allowed to testify without naming evidence to prove that Zola's accusations weren't true. In other words, it was the military's word against Zola's enforced silence.

There was one witness who gave evidence corroborating Zola's facts, Picquart, who was allowed out of prison to appear in court. To refute his testimony, General Georges-Gabriel de Pellieux quoted from the secret dossier, the one forged by Henry and the only proof explicitly naming Dreyfus. When Zola's lawyer demanded the file be put into evidence for review, the military refused, claiming issues of national security. With that, the trial was quickly adjourned and the judges decided against Zola and the managing director of the newspaper. The once-lauded laureate was sentenced to the maximum penalty—a huge fine of 3,000 francs and one year in prison.

Zola demanded a retrial but was found guilty again. Rather than go to prison, he fled to London, where he met Oscar Wilde, just out of jail himself. But the fire that "J'Accuse" had started grew, creating a new Dreyfusard movement and galvanizing public awareness to fight for human rights.

The new Minister of War, Jacques Godefroy Cavaignac, reopened the files, including the secret dossier, and assuming the documents were legitimate, he publicized the contents. Then, too late, he ordered a careful examination of the papers, only to learn that the incriminating pages has been forged by Henry. Henry admitted his guilt and killed himself in his jail cell, providing the Dreyfusards with even more ammunition.

You would think that when a man kills himself over guilt for his crime, the crime he committed would be obvious. But rather than becoming a scapegoat for the army, Henry became a public hero. He was considered someone who had sacrificed himself for his country, and people donated an enormous sum for his widow (130,000 francs) and for a statue to be erected in his honor (still standing in Paris). These donations were often signed with hatred for the Jews. One was "from a future medical student, already sharpening his scalpels to dissect the Maccabee Dreyfus, shot by a dozen bullets from a firing squad." Another was "from a teacher who is sure to tell his students that Jews and their friends are the vampires of France." A third suggested: "finding not enough Jews to massacre, I propose cutting them in two, in order to get twice as many."

Despite the ugly spoutings of anti-Semitism, Henry's suicide created a dramatic change in public opinion. Before his death, only 2 percent of French newspapers were for Dreyfus. Afterward, 40 percent supported him. The Dreyfus Affair divided France, divided families, and severed friendships, as happened with Degas.

With such a strong swell of opinion for Dreyfus's innocence, the government was forced by late 1898 to open yet another judicial process, this time a civilian tribunal. In May 1899, the court concluded that the infamous bordereau was indeed written by Esterházy (who had long since fled to England like his critic, Zola). The judges annulled the 1894 verdict and sent for Dreyfus to answer to a new court-martial.

The response from army supporters was vicious. They accused the justices of being bribed by the imaginary Jewish cabal. The ugly language fostered more turmoil in the streets. Riots broke out and the government collapsed as the prime minister was voted out of office for his failure to deal with the Dreyfus Affair and the military. What Degas had feared came to pass—the military lost stature and the government lost status, both because of Dreyfus. Or actually because of how those two institutions handled the gross injustice they themselves had caused.

The Second Dreyfus Trial

In the summer of 1898, Dreyfus returned from Devil's Island for his new court-martial. Not yet forty, he had aged horribly from malaria and malnutrition. His teeth had rotted out; he'd lost so much weight he looked like a skeleton; and his once black hair had turned white. Because he'd barely spoken to anyone in years, he could only manage a hoarse whisper. Worried that his appearance would make him look sympathetic, the army had a special padded uniform made to disguise how gaunt he was.

This court-martial was very different from the first. Because of assassination threats, Dreyfus was guarded by two hundred mounted police. More than three hundred journalists from all over the world were present. The new invention of the movie camera recorded some of the testimony, leading to one of the first documentaries ever made, *L'Affaire Dreyfus*. (The film was promptly banned by the French government—no film was allowed to made about the Dreyfus Affair in France until 1959.) The courtroom was crammed with as many as a thousand spectators. This trial was a major public event for the entire world and lasted four weeks.

Picquart was freed from prison after nearly a year. Zola returned from England. Both wanted to attend the trial of the century.

But if they expected justice to finally be done, they—and the rest of the world—were disappointed. No military witnesses testified, just the same handwriting expert as before, and the same unproven hearsay evidence was admitted. The crowds were as full of hate and rage as ever.

As Fernand Labori, one of Dreyfus's lawyers, was leaving the courtroom, he was shot in the back. Despite numerous witnesses and all the mounted police, the attacker ran away in the crowd and was never found. Fortunately the injury proved to be minor, and Labori quickly returned to the trial.

The most compelling testimony came from Dreyfus himself, and reporters from all of Europe's newspapers wrote about how clearly the evidence proved him to be innocent. Still, the need to preserve the honor of the military compelled the justices to find Dreyfus guilty again by a vote of five to two. Out of a sense of mercy and given how ill the defendant was, however, they offered to reduce the sentence to only ten years in prison.

Zola wrote in the newspaper *L'Aurore* of the verdict: "there will exist no more detestable monument to human infamy…the ignorance, folly, madness, cruelty, deceit, and crime." He added that this new trial would cause "tomorrow's generations to tremble with shame."

The Fallout

The French press was split in its response, some shamed by how France now looked to the world, others proud of the army and suspicious of the so-called Jewish cabal. The international press was solidly pro-Dreyfus, even in deeply anti-Semitic countries like Russia. In America, Mark Twain skewered France and its farcical claim to have invented the Rights of Man after the French Revolution in admiration of the American Bill of Rights.

Again, riots broke out, and to calm the public and put the

disastrous affair to rest once and for all, the French president pardoned Dreyfus on grounds of ill health and national interest in healing wounds.

The pardon only inflamed public sentiment more. Protests broke out in Chicago, Rome, and London, drawing tens of thousands in support of Dreyfus. Germans warned their citizens not to travel to France, a country where all rights were violated. The British advised that France was no longer a civilized nation.

Zola captured the pervasive sense of despair in the face of such blatant injustice: "I am terrified. What I feel is no longer anger, no longer indignation and the craving to avenge it, no longer the need to denounce a crime and demand its punishment in the name of truth and justice. I am terrified, filled with the sacred awe of a man who witnesses the supernatural: rivers flowing backward toward their sources and the earth toppling over under the sun…for our noble and generous France has fallen to the bottom of the abyss…The world is convinced of Dreyfus's innocence, and France looks ignorant, cruel, blinkered, uncivilized."

Dreyfus was pardoned, though to him liberty was hollow without honor. And in 1900 the National Assembly voted a blanket amnesty to everyone involved in the whole sorry six-year history of the affair. Nobody would ever be held accountable for Dreyfus's suffering or for the suffering of those who supported him, including Picquart and Zola.

When Zola was found dead in his apartment in September 1902, poisoned by fumes from the fireplace, it was immediately suspected that a "patriot" had blocked the chimney, but nothing was ever proved. Dreyfus and his brother both went to the funeral, along with an armed guard, as crowds heckled both the dead writer and the man he'd proclaimed innocent. Zola was buried in an elaborate tomb in Montmartre, but his remains were later moved to a crypt in the Pantheon so he could be honored along with Victor Hugo and Alexandre Dumas, other famous French writers. As Anatole France said of Zola at the funeral, "Fate and courage swept him to the summit, to be, for one moment, the conscience of mankind."

Justice?

Zola was silenced, yet Dreyfus kept pressing for a new judgment, one that would fully exonerate him of all charges. It took twelve years, but in July 1906, the second verdict was annulled and Dreyfus was declared innocent. He was reinstated in the army, promoted to major, and awarded the cross of the Knight of the Legion of Honor in the same War College courtyard where he had been humiliated.

Even after vacating the original judgment against Dreyfus, the government censored public discussion of the affair. No movie on the subject, including anything on the life of Zola, was allowed to be made or shown in France until 1959, when the law was finally changed. The legal reason given for such harshness was the possibility of riots or injury to the honor of the army.

For the same reason, there was no public statue of Dreyfus in Paris until 1985. Even at that late date, the sculpture commissioned by Jack Lang, then Minister of Culture, was considered too controversial for the courtyard of the War College, where it was intended. Almost eighty years after Dreyfus was reinstated, the Army still couldn't accept an image that would remind them of the injustice they had inflicted. A copy was placed in the courtyard of the newly opened Museum of Jewish Art and History, but the original languished in storage for two decades.

Only in 2006, after giving a speech to pacify the military, did President Jacques Chirac have the statue set at the exit to the Notre-Dame-des-Champs metro station. By carefully selecting a site that wasn't too prominent, a place far from the War College, the government at that late date was still choosing military honor over the truth.

The Conscience of Mankind

Despite how immensely important the Dreyfus Affair was, its history is barely known. Reading about it today, the military corruption, the need for a scapegoat, the brutal disrespect for human rights doesn't seem all that distant. This kind of thing could still happen today in this country. Maybe not to a Jew, but maybe to a Muslim this time. And where would we find our Zola?

Bibliography

Burns, Michael. *France and the Dreyfus Affair: A Documentary History*. Boston: Bedford/St. Martin's, 1999.

Clark, T. J. *The Painting of Modern Life: Paris in the Art of Manet and his Followers*. Princeton, NJ: Princeton University Press, 1999.

Dumas, Ann, and Colta Ives, Susan Alyson Stein, and Gary Tinterow. *The Private Collection of Edgar Degas*. New York: The Metropolitan Museum of Art, 1998.

Févre, Jeanne, and Pierre Borel. *Mon Oncle Degas*. New York: Gallery Press, 1949.

Fosca, François. *Degas*. Milan: Skira, 1954.

Guerin, Marcel, ed. *Degas: Letters*. Oxford: Bruno Cassirer, 1947.

Halévy, Daniel, Jean-Pierre Halévy, and Edgar Degas. *Degas Parle*. Paris: Éditions de Fallois, 1960.

Herbert, Robert L. *Impressionism: Art, Leisure, and Parisian Society.* New Haven, CT: Yale University Press, 1991.

Ives Gammell, R. H. *The Shop-Talk of Edgar Degas.* Boston: University Press, 1961.

Nochlin, Linda. *Impressionism & Post-Impressionism, 1874–1904: Sources and Documents.* New York: Prentice Hall, 1966.

———. *Realism & Tradition in Art, 1848–1900: Sources and Documents.* New York: Prentice Hall, 1966.

Paléologue, Maurice. *An Intimate Journal of the Dreyfus Case.* New York: Criterion Books, 1957.

Rewald, John. *The History of Impressionism.* New York: Harry N. Abrams, 1990.

Robb, Graham. *Parisians: An Adventure History of Paris.* New York: W. W. Norton, 2010.

Sutherland Boggs, Jean, and Douglas W. Druick, Henri Loyrette, Michael Pantazzi, and Gary Tinterow. *Degas.* New York: The Metropolitan Museum of Art, 1988.

Vollard, Ambroise. *Degas: An Intimate Portrait.* Sykesville, MD: Greenberg Publisher, 1927.

Whyte, George R. *The Accused: The Dreyfus Trilogy.* Bonn, Germany: Inter Nationes, 1996.

Acknowledgments

I could not have written this book without the help of three superb readers, Asa Stahl, Elias Stahl, and Joan Lester. They waded through a messy first draft to help me give this story the direction it needed. For fine-tuning various revisions I'm grateful to Elisa Kleven, Lisa Kaborycha, and Rob Scheifer. Sometimes it takes a village to make a book.

About the Author

Marissa Moss grew up telling stories and drawing pictures to go with them. She sent her first picture book to publishers when she was nine, but mysteriously enough, never heard back from them. She didn't try again until she was a grown-up, and then it took five years of sending out stories, getting them rejected, revising them, and sending them out again until she got her first book.

Now she's written and illustrated over fifty books. Many of them are from her best-known series, *Amelia's Notebook*. When she wrote the first book fifteen years ago, the format of a hand-written notebook with art on every page was so novel, editors didn't know what to make of it. Now the diary format is a common format.

Mira's Diary: Lost in Paris is another new kind of hybrid book—a mix of history, art, and time travel in the *Amelia* boundary-breaking vein.